When a Man Marries

When a Man Marries
Mary Roberts Rinehart

WILDSIDE PRESS
Doylestown, Pennsylvania

When a Man Marries
A publication of
WILDSIDE PRESS
P.O. Box 301
Holicong, PA 18928-0301
www.wildsidepress.com

Needles and pins
Needles and pins,
When a man marries
His trouble begins.

Chapter I
AT LEAST I MEANT WELL

*W*hen the dreadful thing occurred that night, everyone turned on me. The injustice of it hurt me most. They said I got up the dinner, that I asked them to give up other engagements and come, that I promised all kinds of jollification, if they would come; and then when they did come and got in the papers and everyone — but ourselves — laughed himself black in the face, they turned on *me!* I, who suffered ten times to their one! I shall never forget what Dallas Brown said to me, standing with a coal shovel in one hand and a — well, perhaps it would be better to tell it all in the order it happened.

It began with Jimmy Wilson and a conspiracy, was helped on by a foot-square piece of yellow paper and a Japanese butler, and it enmeshed and mixed up generally ten respectable members of society and a policeman. Incidentally, it involved a pearl collar and a box of soap, which sounds incongruous, doesn't it?

It is a great misfortune to be stout, especially for a man. Jim was rotund and looked shorter than he really was, and as all the lines of his face, or what should have been lines, were really dimples, his face was about as flexible and full of expression as a pillow in a tight cover. The angrier he got the funnier he looked, and when he was raging, and his neck swelled up over his collar and got red, he was entrancing. And everybody liked him, and borrowed money from him, and laughed at his pictures (he has one in the Hargrave gallery in

London now, so people buy them instead), and smoked his cigarettes, and tried to steal his Jap. The whole story hinges on the Jap.

The trouble was, I think, that no one took Jim seriously. His ambition in life was to be taken seriously, but people steadily refused to. His art was a huge joke — except to himself. If he asked people to dinner, everyone expected a frolic. When he married Bella Knowles, people chuckled at the wedding, and considered it the wildest prank of Jimmy's career, although Jim himself seemed to take it awfully hard.

We had all known them both for years. I went to Farmington with Bella, and Anne Brown was her matron of honor when she married Jim. My first winter out, Jimmy had paid me a lot of attention. He painted my portrait in oils and had a studio tea to exhibit it. It was a very nice picture, but it did not look like me, so I stayed away from the exhibition. Jim asked me to. He said he was not a photographer, and that anyhow the rest of my features called for the nose he had given me, and that all the Greuze women have long necks. I have not.

After I had refused Jim twice he met Bella at a camp in the Adirondacks and when he came back he came at once to see me. He seemed to think I would be sorry to lose him, and he blundered over the telling for twenty minutes. Of course, no woman likes to lose a lover, no matter what she may say about it, but Jim had been getting on my nerves for some time, and I was much calmer than he expected me to be.

"If you mean," I said finally in desperation, "that you and Bella are — are in love, why don't you say so, Jim? I think you will find that I stand it wonderfully."

He brightened perceptibly.

"I didn't know how you would take it, Kit," he said, "and I hope we will always be bully friends. You are absolutely sure you don't care a whoop for me?"

"Absolutely," I replied, and we shook hands on it. Then he began about Bella; it was very tiresome.

Bella is a nice girl, but I had roomed with her at school, and I was under no illusions. When Jim raved about Bella and her banjo, and Bella and her guitar, I had painful moments when I recalled Bella, learning her two songs on each instrument, and the old English ballad she had learned to play on the harp. When he said she was too good for him, I never batted an eye. And I shook hands solemnly across the tea-table again, and wished him happiness — which was sincere enough, but hopeless — and said we had only been playing a game, but that it was time to stop playing. Jim kissed my hand, and it was really very touching.

We had been the best of friends ever since. Two days before the wedding he came around from his tailor's, and we burned all his letters to me. He would read one and say: "Here's a crackerjack, Kit," and pass it to me. And after I had read it we would lay it on the fire log, and Jim would say, "I am not worthy of her, Kit. I wonder if I can make her happy?" Or — "Did you know that the Duke of Belford proposed to her in London last winter?"

Of course, one has to take the woman's word about a thing like that, but the Duke of Belford had been mad about Maude Richard all that winter.

You can see that the burning of the letters, which was meant to be reminiscently sentimental, a sort of how-silly-we-were-but-it-is-all-over-now occasion, became actually a two hours' eulogy of Bella. And just when I was bored to death, the Mercer girls dropped in and heard Jim begin to read one commencing "dearest Kit." And the next day after the rehearsal dinner, they told Bella!

There was very nearly no wedding at all. Bella came to see me in a frenzy the next morning and threw Jim and his two-hundred odd pounds in my face, and although I explained it all over and over, she never quite forgave me. That was what made it so hard later — the situation would have been bad enough without that complication.

They went abroad on their wedding journey, and stayed several months. And when Jim came back he was fatter than ever. Everybody noticed it. Bella had a gymnasium fitted up in a corner of the studio, but he would not use it. He smoked a pipe and painted all day, and drank beer and *would* eat starches or whatever it is that is fattening. But he adored Bella, and he was madly jealous of her. At dinners he used to glare at the man who took her in, although it did not make him thin. Bella was flirting, too, and by the time they had been married a year, people hitched their chairs together and dropped their voices when they were mentioned.

Well, on the anniversary of the day Bella left him — oh yes, she left him finally. She was intense enough about some things, and she said it got on her nerves to have everybody chuckle when they asked for her husband. They would say, "Hello, Bella! How's Bubbles? Still banting?" And Bella would try to laugh and say, "He swears his tailor says his waist is smaller, but if it is he must be growing hollow in the back."

But she got tired of it at last. Well, on the second anniversary of Bella's departure, Jimmy was feeling pretty glum, and as I say, I am very fond of Jim. The divorce had just gone through and Bella had taken her maiden name again and had had an operation for appendicitis. We heard afterward that they didn't find an appendix, and that the one they showed her in a glass jar *was not hers!* But if Bella ever suspected, she didn't say. Whether the appendix was anonymous or not, she got box after box of flowers that were, and of course everyone knew that it was Jim who sent them.

To go back to the anniversary, I went to Rothberg's to see the collection of antique furniture — mother was looking for a sideboard for father's birthday in March — and I met Jimmy there, boring into a worm-hole in a seventeenth-century bedpost with the end of a match, and looking his nearest to sad. When he saw me he came over.

"I'm blue today, Kit," he said, after we had shaken hands. "Come and help me dig bait, and then let's go fishing. If there's a worm in every hole in that bedpost, we could go into the fish business. It's a good business."

"Better than painting?" I asked. But he ignored my gibe and swelled up alarmingly in order to sigh.

"This is the worst day of the year for me," he affirmed, staring straight ahead, "and the longest. Look at that crazy clock over there. If you want to see your life passing away, if you want to see the steps by which you are marching to eternity, watch that clock marking the time. Look at that infernal hand staying quiet for sixty seconds and then jumping forward to catch up with the procession. Ugh!"

"See here, Jim," I said, leaning forward, "you're not well. You can't go through the rest of the day like this. I know what you'll do; you'll go home to play Grieg on the pianola, and you won't eat any dinner." He looked guilty.

"Not Grieg," he protested feebly. "Beethoven."

"You're not going to do either," I said with firmness. "You are going right home to unpack those new draperies that Harry Bayles sent you from Shanghai, and you are going to order dinner for eight — that will be two tables of bridge. And you are not going to touch the pianola."

He did not seem enthusiastic, but he rose and picked up his hat, and stood looking down at me where I sat on an old horse-hair covered sofa.

"I wish to thunder I had married you!" he said savagely. "You're the finest girl I know, Kit, *without exception,* and you are going to throw yourself away on Jack Manning, or Max, or some other —"

"Nothing of the sort," I said coldly, "and the fact that you didn't marry me does not give you the privilege of abusing my friends. Anyhow, I don't like you when you speak like that."

Jim took me to the door and stopped there to sigh.

"I haven't been well," he said heavily. "Don't eat, don't sleep. Wouldn't you think I'd lose flesh? Kit" — he lowered his voice solemnly — "I have gained two pounds!"

I said he didn't look it, which appeared to comfort him somewhat, and, because we were old friends, I asked him where Bella was. He said he thought she was in Europe, and that he had heard she was going to marry Reggie Wolfe. Then he signed again, muttered something about ordering the funeral baked meats to be prepared and left me.

That was my entire share in the affair. I was the victim, both of circumstances and of their plot, which was mad on the face of it.

During the entire time they never once let me forget that I got up the dinner, that I telephoned around for them. They asked me why I couldn't cook — when not one of them knew one side of a range from the other. And for Anne Brown to talk the way she did — saying I had always been crazy about Jim, and that she believed I had known all along that his aunt was coming — for Anne to talk like that was sheer idiocy. Yes, there was an aunt. The Japanese butler started the trouble, and Aunt Selina carried it along.

Chapter II
THE WAY IT BEGAN

*I*t makes me angry every time I think how I tried to make that dinner a success. I canceled a theater engagement, and I took the Mercer girls in the electric brougham father had given me for Christmas. Their chauffeur had been gone for hours with their machine, and they had telephoned all the police stations without success. They were afraid that there had been an awful smash; they could easily have replaced Bartlett, as Lollie said, but it takes so long to get new parts for those foreign cars.

Jim had a house well up-town, and it stood just enough apart from the other houses to be entirely maddening later. It was a three-story affair, with a basement kitchen and servants' dining room. Then, of course, there were cellars, as we found out afterward. On the first floor there was a large square hall, a formal reception room, behind it a big living room that was also a library, then a den, and back of all a Georgian dining room, with windows high above the ground. On the top floor Jim had a studio, like every other one I ever saw — perhaps a little mussier. Jim was really a grind at his painting, and there were cigarette ashes and palette knives and buffalo rugs and shields everywhere. It is strange, but when I think of that terrible house, I always see the halls, enormous, covered with heavy rugs, and stairs that would have taken six housemaids to keep in proper condition. I dream about those stairs, stretching above me in a Jacob's ladder of shining wood and Persian carpets, going up, up, clear to the roof.

The Dallas Browns walked; they lived in the next block. And they brought with them a man named Harbison, that no one knew. Anne said he would be great sport, because he was terribly serious, and had the most exaggerated ideas of society, and loathed extravagance, and built bridges or something. She had put away her cigarettes since he had been with them — he and Dallas had been college friends — and the only chance she had to smoke was when she was getting her hair done. And she had singed off quite a lot — a burned offering, she called it.

"My dear," she said over the telephone, when I invited her, "I want you to know him. He'll be crazy about you. That type of man, big and deadly earnest, always falls in love with your type of girl, the appealing sort, you know. And he has been too busy, up to now, to know what love is. But mind, don't hurt him; he's a dear boy. I'm half in love with him myself, and Dallas trots around at his heels like a poodle."

But all Anne's geese are swans, so I thought little of the Harbison man except to hope that he played respectable bridge, and wouldn't mark the cards with a steel spring under his finger nail, as one of her "finds" had done.

We all arrived about the same time, and Anne and I went upstairs together to take off our wraps in what had been Bella's dressing room. It was Anne who noticed the violets.

"Look at that!" she nudged me, when the maid was examining her wrap before she laid it down. "What did I tell you, Kit? He's still quite mad about her."

Jim had painted Bella's portrait while they were going up the Nile on their wedding trip. It looked quite like her, if you stood well off in the middle of the room and if the light came from the right. And just beneath it, in a silver vase, was a bunch of violets. It was really touching, and violets were fabulous. It made me want to cry, and to shake Bella soundly, and to go down and pat Jim on his generous shoulder, and tell him what a good fellow I thought him, and that Bella wasn't worth the dust under his feet. I don't know much about psychology, but it would be interesting to know just what effect those violets and my sympathy for Jim had in influencing my decision a half hour later. It is not surprising, under the circumstances, that for some time after the odor of violets made me ill.

We all met downstairs in the living room, quite informally, and Dallas was banging away at the pianola, tramping the pedals with the delicacy and feeling of a football center rush kicking a goal. Mr. Harbison was standing near the fire, a little away from the others, and he was all that Anne had said and more in appearance. He was tall — not too tall, and very straight. And after one got past the oddity of his face being bronze-colored above his white collar, and of his brown hair being sun-bleached on top until it was almost yellow, one realized that he was very handsome. He had what one might call a resolute nose and chin, and a pleasant, rather humorous, mouth. And he had blue eyes that were, at that moment, wandering with interest over the lot of us. Somebody shouted his name to me above the Tristan and Isolde music, and I held out my hand.

Instantly I had the feeling one sometimes has, of having done just that same thing, with the same surroundings, in the same place, years before, I was looking up at him, and he was staring down at me and holding my hand. And then the music stopped and he was saying:

"Where was it?"

"Where was what?" I asked. The feeling was stronger than ever with his voice.

"I beg your pardon," he said, and let my hand drop. "Just for a second I had an idea that we had met before somewhere, a long time ago. I suppose — no, it couldn't have happened, or I should remember." He was smiling, half at himself.

"No," I smiled back at him. "It didn't happen, I'm afraid — unless we dreamed it."

"We?"

"I felt that way, too, for a moment."

"The Brushwood Boy!" he said with conviction. "Perhaps we will find a common dream life, where we knew each other. You remember the Brushwood Boy loved the girl for years before they really met." But this was a little too rapid, even for me.

"Nothing so sentimental, I'm afraid," I retorted. "I have had exactly the same sensation sometimes when I have sneezed."

Betty Mercer captured him then and took him off to see
Jim's newest picture. Anne pounced on me at once.

"Isn't he delicious?" she demanded. "Did you ever see such
shoulders? And such a nose? And he thinks we are parasites,
cumberers of the earth, Heaven knows what. He says every
woman ought to know how to earn her living, in case of
necessity! I said I could make enough at bridge, and he
thought I was joking! He's a dear!" Anne was enthusiastic.

I looked after him. Oddly enough the feeling that we had
met before stuck to me. Which was ridiculous, of course, for
we learned afterward that the nearest we ever came to meeting
was that our mothers had been school friends! Just then I saw
Jim beckoning to me crazily from the den. He looked quite
yellow, and he had been running his fingers through his hair.

"For Heaven's sake, come in, Kit!" he said. "I need a cool
head. Didn't I tell you this is my calamity day?"

"Cook gone?" I asked with interest. I was starving.

He closed the door and took up a tragic attitude in front
of the fire. "Did you ever hear of Aunt Selina?" he demanded.

"I knew there *was* one," I ventured, mindful of certain
gossip as to whence Jimmy derived the Wilson income.

Jim himself was too worried to be cautious. He waved a
brazen hand at the snug room, at the Japanese prints on the
walls, at the rugs, at the teakwood cabinets and the screen
inlaid with pearl and ivory.

"All this," he said comprehensively, "every bite I eat,
clothes I wear, drinks I drink — you needn't look like that; I
don't drink so darned much — everything comes from Aunt
Selina — buttons," he finished with a groan.

"Selina Buttons," I said reflectively. "I don't remember ever
having known anyone named Buttons, although I had a cat
once —"

"Damn the cat!" he said rudely. "Her name isn't Buttons.
Her name is Caruthers, my Aunt Selina Caruthers, and the
money comes from buttons."

"Oh!" feebly.

"It's an old business," he went on, with something of
proprietary pride. "My grandfather founded it in 1775. Made
buttons for the Continental Army."

"Oh, yes," I said. "They melted the buttons to make bullets, didn't they? Or they melted bullets to make buttons? Which was it?"

But again he interrupted.

"It's like this," he went on hurriedly. "Aunt Selina believes in me. She likes pictures, and she wanted me to paint, if I could. I'd have given up long ago — oh, I know what you think of my work — but for Aunt Selina. She has encouraged me, and she's done more than that; she's paid the bills."

"Dear Aunt Selina," I breathed.

"When I got married," Jim persisted, "Aunt Selina doubled my allowance. I always expected to sell something, and begin to make money, and in the meantime what she advanced I considered as a loan." He was eyeing me defiantly, but I was growing serious. It was evident from the preamble that something was coming.

"To understand, Kit," he went on dubiously, "you would have to know her. She won't stand for divorce. She thinks it is a crime."

"What!" I sat up. I have always regarded divorce as essentially disagreeable, like castor oil, but necessary.

"Oh, you know well enough what I'm driving at," he burst out savagely. "She doesn't know Bella has gone. She thinks I am living in a little domestic heaven, and — she is coming tonight to hear me flap my wings."

"Tonight!"

I don't think Jimmy had known that Dallas Brown had come in and was listening. I am sure I had not. Hearing his chuckle at the doorway brought us up with a jerk.

"Where has Aunt Selina been for the last two or three years?" he asked easily.

Jim turned, and his face brightened.

"Europe. Look here, Dal, you're a smart chap. She'll only be here about four hours. Can't you think of some way to get me out of this? I want to let her down easy, too. I'm mighty fond of Aunt Selina. Can't we — can't I say Bella has a headache?"

"Rotten!" laconically.

"Gone out of town?" Jim was desperate.

"And you with a houseful of dinner guests! Try again, Jim."

"I have it," Jim said suddenly. "Dallas, ask Anne if she

won't play hostess for tonight. Be Mrs. Wilson pro tem. Anne would love it. Aunt Selina never saw Bella. Then, afterward, next year, when I'm hung in the Academy and can stand on my feet" — ("Not if you're hung," Dallas interjected.) — "I'll break the truth to her."

But Dallas was not enthusiastic.

"Anne wouldn't do at all," he declared. "She'd be talking about the kids before she knew it, and patting me on the head." He said it complacently; Anne flirts, but they are really devoted.

"One of the Mercer girls?" I suggested, but Jimmy raised a horrified hand.

"You don't know Aunt Selina," he protested. "I couldn't offer Leila in the gown she's got on, unless she wore a shawl, and Betty is too fair."

Anne came in just then, and the whole story had to be told again to her. She was ecstatic. She said it was good enough for a play, and that of course she would be Mrs. Jimmy for that length of time.

"You know," she finished, "if it were not for Dal, I would be Mrs. Jimmy for *any* length of time. I have been devoted to you for years, Billiken."

But Dallas refused peremptorily.

"I'm not jealous," he explained, straightening and throwing out his chest, "but — well, you don't look the part Anne. You're — you are growing matronly, not but what you suit *me* all right. And then I'd forget and call you 'mammy,' which would require explanation. I think it's up to you, Kit."

"I shall do nothing of the sort!" I snapped. "It's ridiculous!"

"I dare you!" said Dallas.

I refused. I stood like a rock while the storm surged around me and beat over me. I must say for Jim that he was merely pathetic. He said that my happiness was first; that he would not give me an uncomfortable minute for anything on earth; and that Bella had been perfectly right to leave him, because he was a sinking ship, and deserved to be turned out penniless into the world. After which mixed figure, he poured himself something to drink, and his hands were shaking.

Dal and Anne stood on each side of him and patted him

on the shoulders and glared across at me. I felt that if I was a rock, Jim's ship had struck on me and was sinking, as he said, because of me. I began to crumble.

"What — what time does she leave?" I asked, wavering.

"Ten: nine; *Kit,* are you going to do it?"

"No!" I gave a last clutch at my resolution. "People who do that kind of thing always get into trouble. She might miss her train. She's almost certain to miss her train."

"You're temporizing," Dallas said sternly. "We won't let her miss her train; you can be sure of that."

"Jim," Anne broke in suddenly, "hasn't she a picture of Bella? There's not the faintest resemblance between Bella and Kit."

Jim became downcast again. "I sent her a miniature of Bella a couple of years ago," he said despondently. "Did it myself."

But Dal said he remembered the miniature, and it looked more like me than Bella, anyhow. So we were just where we started. And down inside of me I had a premonition that I was going to do just what they wanted me to do, and get into all sorts of trouble, and not be thanked for it after all. Which was entirely correct. And then Leila Mercer came and banged at the door and said that dinner had been announced ages ago and that everybody was famishing. With the hurry and stress, and poor Jim's distracted face, I weakened.

"I feel like a cross between an idiot and a criminal," I said shortly, "and I don't know particularly why everyone thinks I should be the victim for the sacrifice. But if you will promise to get her off early to her train, and if you will stand by me and not leave me alone with her, I — I might try it."

"Of course, we'll stand by you!" they said in chorus. "We won't let you stick!" And Dal said, "You're the right sort of girl, Kit. And after it's all over, you'll realize that it's the biggest kind of lark. Think how you are saving the old lady's feeling! When you are an elderly person yourself, Kit, you will appreciate what you are doing tonight."

Yes, they said they would stand by me, and that I was a heroine and the only person there clever enough to act the part, and that they wouldn't let me stick! I am not bitter now, but that is what they promised. Oh, I am not defending myself; I suppose I deserved everything that happened. But they told me that she would be there only between trains, and that she was deaf, and that I had an opportunity to save a fellow-being from ruin. So in the end I capitulated.

When they opened the door into the living room, Max Reed had arrived and was helping to hide a decanter and glasses, and somebody said a cab was at the door.

And that was the way it began.

Chapter III
I MIGHT HAVE KNOWN IT

*T*he minute I had consented I regretted it. After all, what were Jimmy's troubles to me? Why should I help him impose on an unsuspecting elderly woman? And it was only putting off discovery anyhow. Sooner or later, she would learn of the divorce, and — Just at that instant my eyes fell on Mr. Harbison — Tom Harbison, as Anne called him. He was looking on with an amused, half-puzzled smile, while people were rushing around hiding the roulette wheel and things of which Miss Caruthers might disapprove, and Betty Mercer was on her knees winding up a toy bear that Max had brought her. What would he think? It was evident that he thought badly of us already — that he was contemptuously amused, and then to have to ask him to lend himself to the deception!

With a gasp I hurled myself after Jimmy, only to hear a strange voice in the hall and to know that I was too late. I was in for it, whatever was coming. It was Aunt Selina who was coming — along the hall, followed by Jim, who was mopping his face and trying not to notice the paralyzed silence in the library.

Aunt Selina met me in the doorway. To my frantic eyes she seemed to tower above us by at least a foot, and beside her Jimmy was a red, perspiring cherub.

"Here she is," Jimmy said, from behind a temporary eclipse of black cloak and traveling bag. He was on top of the situation now, and he was mendaciously cheerful. He had *not* said, "Here is my wife." That would have been a lie. No,

Jimmy merely said, "Here she is." If Aunt Selina chose to think me Bella, was it not her responsibility? And if I chose to accept the situation, was it not mine? Dallas Brown came forward gravely as Aunt Selina folded over and kissed me, and surreptitiously patted me with one hand while he held out the other to Miss Caruthers. I loathed him!

"We always expect something unusual from James, Miss Caruthers," he said, with his best manner, "but *this* — this is beyond our wildest dreams."

Well, it's too awful to linger over. Anne took her upstairs and into Bella's bedroom. It was a fancy of Jim's to leave that room just as Bella had left it, dusty dance cards and favors hanging around and a pair of discarded slippers under the bed. I don't think it had been swept since Bella left it. I believe in sentiment, but I like it brushed and dusted and the cobwebs off of it, and when Aunt Selina put down her bonnet, it stirred up a gray-white cloud that made her cough. She did not say anything, but she looked around the room grimly, and I saw her run her finger over the back of a chair before she let Hannah, the maid, put her cloak on it.

Anne looked frightened. She ran into Bella's bath and wet the end of a towel and when Hannah was changing Aunt Selina's collar — her concession to evening dress — Anne wiped off the obvious places on the furniture. She did it stealthily, but Aunt Selina saw her in the glass.

"What's that young woman's name?" she asked me sharply, when Anne had taken the towel out to hide it.

"Anne Brown, Mrs. Dallas Brown," I replied meekly. Everyone replied meekly to Aunt Selina.

"Does she live here?"

"Oh, no," I said airily. "They are here to dinner, she and her husband. They are old friends of Jim's — and mine."

"Seems to have a good eye for dirt," said Aunt Selina and went on fastening her brooch. When she was finally ready, she took a bead purse from somewhere about her waist and took out a half dollar. She held it up before Hannah's eyes.

"Tomorrow morning," she said sternly, "You take off that white cap and that *fol-de-rol* apron and that black henrietta cloth, and put on a calico wrapper. And when you've got this room aired and swept, Mrs. Wilson will give you this."

Hannah took two steps back and caught hold of a chair; she stared helplessly from Aunt Selina to the half dollar, and then at me. Anne was trying not to catch my eye.

"And another thing," Aunt Selina said, from the head of the stairs, "I sent those towels over from Ireland. Tell her to wash and bleach the one Mrs. What's-her-name Brown used as a duster."

Anne was quite crushed as we went down the stairs. I turned once, half-way down, and her face was a curious mixture of guilt and hopeless wrath. Over her shoulder, I could see Hannah, wide-eyed and puzzled, staring after us.

Jim presented everybody, and then he went into the den and closed the door and we heard him unlock the cellaret. Aunt Selina looked at Leila's bare shoulders and said she guessed she didn't take cold easily, and conversation rather languished. Max Reed was looking like a thundercloud, and he came over to me with a lowering expression that I had learned to dread in him.

"What fool nonsense is this?" he demanded. "What in the world possessed you, Kit, to put yourself in such an equivocal position? Unless" — he stopped and turned a little white — "unless you are going to marry Jim."

I am sorry for Max. He is such a nice boy, and good looking, too, if only he were not so fierce, and did not want to make love to me. No matter what I do, Max always disapproves of it. I have always had a deeply rooted conviction that if I should ever in a weak moment marry Max, he would disapprove of that, too, before I had done it very long.

"Are you?" he demanded, narrowing his eyes — a sign of unusually bad humor.

"Am I what?"

"Going to marry him?"

"If you mean Jim," I said with dignity, "I haven't made up my mind yet. Besides, he hasn't asked me."

Aunt Selina had been talking Woman's Suffrage in front of the fireplace, but now she turned to me.

"Is this the vase Cousin Jane Whitcomb sent you as a wedding present?" she demanded, indicating a hideous urn-shaped affair on the mantel. It came to me as an inspiration that Jim had once said it was an ancestral urn, so I said without hesitation that it was. And because there was a pause and everyone was looking at us, I added that it was a beautiful thing.

Aunt Selina sniffed.

"Hideous!" she said. "It looks like Cousin Jane, shape and coloring."

Then she looked at it more closely, pounced on it, turned it upside down and shook it. A card fell out, which Dallas picked up and gave her with a bow. Jim had come out of the den and was dancing wildly around and beckoning to me. By the time I had made out that that was *not* the vase Cousin Jane had sent us as a wedding present, Aunt Selina had examined the card. Then she glared across at me and, stooping, put the card in the fire. I did not understand at all, but I knew I had in some way done the unforgivable thing. Later, Dal told me it was *her* card, and that she had sent the vase to Jim at Christmas, with a generous check inside. When she straightened from the fireplace, it was to a new theme, which she attacked with her usual vigor. The vase incident was over, but she never forgot it. She proved that she never did when she sent me two urn-shaped vases with Paul and Virginia on them, when I — that is, later on.

"The Cause in England has made great strides," she announced from the fireplace. "Soon the hand that rocks the cradle will be the hand that actually rules the world." Here she looked at me.

"I'm not up on such things," Max said blandly, having recovered some of his good humor, "but — isn't it usually a foot that rocks the cradle?"

Aunt Selina turned on him and Mr. Harbison, who were standing together, with a snort.

"What have you, or *you*, ever done for the independence of woman?" she demanded.

Mr. Harbison smiled. He had been looking rather grave until then. "We have at least remained unmarried," he retorted. And then dinner was again announced.

He was to take me out, and he came across the room to where I sat collapsed in a chair, and bent over me.

"Do you know," he said, looking down at me with his clear, disconcerting gaze, "do you know that I have just grasped the situation? There was such a noise that I did not hear your name, and I am only realizing now that you are my hostess! I don't know why I got the impression that this was a bachelor establishment, but I did. Odd, wasn't it?"

I positively couldn't look away from him. My features seemed frozen, and my eyes were glued to his. As for telling him the truth — well, my tongue refused to move. I intended to tell him during dinner if I had an opportunity; I honestly did. But the more I looked at him and saw how candid his eyes were, and how stern his mouth might be, the more I shivered at the plunge. And, of course, as everybody knows now, I didn't tell him at all. And every moment I expected that awful old woman to ask me what I paid my cook, and when I had changed the color of my hair — Bella's being black.

Dinner was a half hour late when we finally went out, Jimmy leading off with Aunt Selina, and I, as hostess, trailing behind the procession with Mr. Harbison. Dallas took in the two Mercer girls, for we were one man short, and Max took Anne. Leila Mercer was so excited that she wriggled, and as for me, the candles and the orchids — everything — danced around in a circle, and I just seemed to catch the back of my chair as it flew past. Jim had ordered away the wines and brought out some weak and cheap Chianti. Dallas looked gloomy at the change, but Jim explained in an undertone that Aunt Selina didn't approve of expensive vintages. Naturally, the meal was glum enough.

Aunt Selina had had her dinner on the train, so she spent her time in asking me questions the length of the table, and in getting acquainted with me. She had brought a bottle of some sort of medicine downstairs with her, and she took a claret-glassful, while she talked. The stuff was called Pomona; shall I ever forget it?

It was Mr. Harbison who first noticed Takahiro. Jimmy's Jap had been the only thing in the ménage that Bella declared she had hated to leave. But he was doing the strangest things: his little black eyes shifted nervously, and he looked queer.

"What's wrong with him?" Mr. Harbison asked me finally, when he saw that I noticed. "Is he ill?"

Then Aunt Selina's voice from the other end of the table: "Bella," she called, in a high shrill tone, "do you let James eat cucumbers?"

"I think he must be," I said hurriedly aside to Mr. Harbison. "See how his hands shake!" But Selina would not be ignored.

"Cucumbers and strawberries," she repeated impressively. "I was saying, Bella, that cucumbers have always given James the most fearful indigestion. And yet I see you serve them at your table. Do you remember what I wrote you to give him when he has his dreadful spells?"

I was quite speechless; everyone was looking, and no one could help. It was clear Jim was racking his brain, and we sat staring desperately at each other across the candles. Everything I had ever known faded from me, eight pairs of eyes bored into me, Mr. Harbison's politely amused.

"I don't remember," I said at last. "Really, I don't believe —" Aunt Selina smiled in a superior way.

"Now, don't you recall it?" she insisted. "I said: 'Baking soda in water taken internally for cucumbers; baking soda and water externally, rubbed on, when he gets that dreadful, itching strawberry rash.'"

I believe the dinner went on. Somebody asked Aunt Selina how much overcharge she had paid in foreign hotels, and after that she was as harmless as a dove.

Then half way through the dinner we heard a crash in Takahiro's pantry, and when he did not appear again, Jim got up and went out to investigate. He was gone quite a little while, and when he came back he looked worried.

"Sick," he replied to our inquiring glances. "One of the maids will come in. They have sent for a doctor."

Aunt Selina was for going out at once and "fixing him up," as she put it, but Dallas gently interfered.

"I wouldn't, Miss Caruthers," he said, in the deferential manner he had adopted toward her. "You don't know what it may be. He's been looking spotty all evening."

"It might be scarlet fever," Max broke in cheerfully. "I say, scarlet fever on a Mongolian — what color would he be, Jimmy? What do yellow and red make? Green?"

"Orange," Jim said shortly. "I wish you people would remember that we are trying to eat."

The fact was, however, that no one was really eating, except

Mr. Harbison who had given up trying to understand us, considering, no doubt, our subdued excitement as our normal condition. Ages afterward I learned that he thought my face almost tragic that night, and that he supposed from the way I glared across the table, that I had quarreled with my husband!

"I am afraid you are not well," he said at last, noticing my food untouched on my plate. "We should not have come, any of us."

"I am perfectly well,:" I replied feverishly. "I am never ill. I — I ate a late luncheon."

He glanced at me keenly. "Don't let them stay and play bridge tonight," he urged. "Miss Caruthers can be an excuse, can she not? And you are really fagged. You look it."

"I think it is only ill humor," I said, looking directly at him. "I am angry at myself. I have done something silly, and I hate to be silly."

Max would have said "Impossible," or something else trite. The Harbison man looked at me with interested, serious eyes.

"Is it too late to undo it?" he asked.

And then and there I determined that he should never know the truth. He could go back to South America and build bridges and make love to the Spanish girls (or are they Spanish down there?) and think of me always as a married woman, married to a dilettante artist, inclined to be stout — the artist, not I — and with an Aunt Selina Caruthers who made buttons and believed in the Cause. But never, *never* should he think of me as a silly little fool who pretended that she was the other man's wife and had a lump in her throat because when a really nice man came along, a man who knew something more than polo and motors, she had to carry on the deception to keep his respect, and be sedate and matronly, and see him change from perfect open admiration at first to a hands-off-she-is-my-host's-wife attitude at last.

"It can never be undone," I said soberly.

Well, that's the picture as nearly as I can draw it: a round table with a low centerpiece of orchids in lavenders and pink, old silver candlesticks with filigree shades against the somber wainscoting; nine people, two of them unhappy — Jim and I; one of them complacent — Aunt Selina; one puzzled — Mr.

Harbison; and the rest hysterically mirthful. Add one sick
Japanese butler and grind in the mills of the gods.

Everyone promptly forgot Takahiro in the excitement of
the game we were all playing. Finally, however, Aunt Selina,
who seemed to have Takahiro on her mind, looked up from
her plate.

"That Jap was speckled," she asserted. "I wouldn't be surprised if it's measles. Has he been sniffling, James?"

"Has he been sniffling?" Jim threw across at me.

"I hadn't noticed it," I said meekly, while the others
choked.

Max came to the rescue. "She refused to eat it," he explained, distinctly and to everybody, apropos absolutely of
nothing. "It said on the box, 'ready cooked and predigested.'
She declared she didn't care who cooked it, but she wanted
to know who predigested it."

As everyone wanted to laugh, everyone did it then, and
under cover of the noise I caught Anne's eye, and we left the
dining room. The men stayed, and by the very firmness with
which the door closed behind us, I knew that Dallas and Max
were bringing out the bottles that Takahiro had hidden. I was
seething. When Aunt Selina indicated a desire to go over the
house (it was natural that she should want to; it was her house,
in a way) I excused myself for a minute and flew back to the
dining room.

It was as I had expected. Jim hadn't cheered perceptibly,
and the rest were patting him on the back, and pouring things
out for him, and saying, "Poor old Jim" in the most maddening way. And the Harbison man was looking more and more
puzzled, and not at all hilarious.

I descended on them like a thunderbolt.

"That's it,:" I cried shrewishly, with my back against the
door. "Leave her to me, all of you, and pat each other on the
back, and say it's gone splendidly! Oh, I know you, everyone!"
Mr. Harbison got up and pulled out a chair, but I couldn't
sit; I folded my arms on the back. "After a while, I suppose,
you'll slip upstairs, the four of you, and have your game."
They looked guilty. "But I will block that right now. I am
going to stay — here. If Aunt Selina wants me, she can find
me — here!"

The first indication those men had that Mr. Harbison didn't know the state of affairs was when he turned and faced them.

"Mrs. Wilson is quite right," he said gravely. "We're a selfish lot. If Miss Caruthers is a responsibility, let us share her."

"To arms!" Jim said, with an affectation of lightness, as they put their glasses down, and threw open the door. Dal's retort, "Whose?" was lost in the confusion, and we went into the library. On the way Dallas managed to speak to me.

"If Harbison doesn't know, don't tell him," he said in an undertone. "He's a queer duck, in some ways; he mightn't think it funny."

"Funny," I choked. "It's the least funny thing I ever experienced. Deceiving that Harbison man isn't so bad — he thinks me crazy, anyhow. He's been staring his eyes out at me —"

"I don't wonder. You're really lovely tonight, Kit, and you look like a vixen."

"But to deceive that harmless old lady — well, thank goodness, it's nine, and she leaves in an hour or so."

But she didn't and that's the story.

Chapter IV

THE DOOR WAS CLOSED

*I*t was infuriating to see how much enjoyment everyone but Jim and myself got out of the situation. They howled with mirth over the feeblest jokes, and when Max told a story without any point whatever, they all had hysteria. Immediately after dinner Aunt Selina had begun on the family connection again, and after two bad breaks on my part, Jim offered to show her the house. The Mercer girls trailed along, unwilling to lose any of the possibilities. They said afterward that it was terrible: she went into all the closets, and ran her hand over the tops of doors and kept getting grimmer and grimmer. In the studio they came across a life study Jim was doing and she shut her eyes and made the girls go out while he covered it with a drapery. Lollie! Who did the Bacchante dance at three benefits last winter and was learning a new one called "Eve!"

When they heard Aunt Selina on the second floor, Anne, Dal and Max sneaked up to the studio for cigarettes, which left Mr. Harbison to me. I was in the den, sitting in a low chair by the wood fire when he came in. He hesitated in the doorway.

"Would you prefer being alone, or may I come in?" he asked. "Don't mind being frank. I know you are tired."

"I have a headache, and I am sulking," I said unpleasantly, "but at least I am not actively venomous. Come in."

So he came in and sat down across the hearth from me, and neither of us said anything. The firelight flickered over the room, bringing out the faded hues of the old Japanese prints on the walls, gleaming in the mother-of-pearl eyes of the dragon on the screen, setting a grotesque god on a cabinet to nodding. And it threw into relief the strong profile of the man across from me, as he stared at the fire.

"I am afraid I am not very interesting," I said at last, when he showed no sign of breaking the silence. "The — the illness of the butler and — Miss Caruthers' arrival, have been upsetting."

He suddenly roused with a start from a brown reverie.

"I beg your pardon," he said, "I — oh, of course not! I was wondering if I — if you were offended at what I said earlier in the evening; the — Brushwood Boy, you know, and all that."

"Offended?" I repeated, puzzled.

"You see, I have been living out of the world so long, and never seeing any women but Indian squaws" — so there were no Spanish girls! — "that I'm afraid I say what comes into my mind without circumlocution. And then — I did not know you were married."

"No, oh, no," I said hastily. "But, of course, the more a woman is married — I mean, you can not say too many nice things to married women. They — need them, you know."

I had floundered miserably, with his eyes on me, and I half expected him to be shocked, or to say that married women should be satisfied with the nice things their husbands say to them. But he merely remarked apropos of nothing, or following a line of thought he had not voiced, that it was trite but true that a good many men owed their success in life to their wives.

"And a good many owe their wives to their success in life," I retorted cynically. At which he stared at me again.

It was then that the real complexity of the situation began to develop. Some one had rung the bell and been admitted to the library and a maid came to the door of the den. When she saw us she stopped uncertainly. Even then it struck me that she looked odd, and she was not in uniform. However, I was not informed at that time about bachelor establishments, and the first thing she said, when she had asked to speak to me in the hall, knocked her and her clothes clear out of my head. Evidently she knew me.

"Miss McNair," she said in a low tone. "There is a lady in the drawing room, a veiled person, and she is asking for Mr. Wilson."

"Can you not find him?" I asked. "He is in the house, probably in the studio."

The girl hesitated.

"Excuse me, miss, but Miss Caruthers —"

Then I saw the situation.

"Never mind," I said. "Close the door into the drawing room, and I will tell Mr. Wilson."

But as the girl turned toward the doorway, the person in question appeared in it, and raised her veil. I was perfectly paralyzed. It was Bella! Bella in a fur coat and a veil, with the most tragic eyes I ever saw and entirely white except for a dab of rouge in the middle of each cheek. We stared at each other without speech. The maid turned and went down the hall, and with that Bella came over to me and clutched me by the arm.

"Who was being carried out into that ambulance?" she demanded, glaring at me with the most awful intensity.

"I'm sure I don't know, Bella," I said, wriggling away from her fingers. "What in the world are you doing here? I thought you were in Europe."

"You are hiding something from me!" she accused. "It is Jim! I see it in your face."

"Well, it isn't," I snapped. "It seems to me, really, Bella, that you and Jim ought to be able to manage your own affairs, without dragging me in." It was not pleasant, but if she was suffering, so was I. "Jim is as well as he ever was. He's upstairs somewhere. I'll send for him."

She gripped me again, and held on while her color came back.

"You'll do nothing of the kind," she said, and she had quite got hold of herself again. "I do not want to see him: I hope you don't think, Kit, that I came here to see James Wilson. Why, I have forgotten that there *is* such a person, and you know it."

Somebody upstairs laughed, and I was growing nervous. What if Aunt Selina should come down, or Mr. Harbison come out of the den?

"Why *did* you come, then, Bella?" I inquired. "He may come in."

"I was passing in the motor," she said, and I honestly think she hoped I would believe her, "and I saw that am —" She stopped and began again. "I thought Jim was out of town, and I came to see Takahiro," she said brazenly. "He was devoted to me, and Evans is going to leave. I'll tell you what to do, Kit. I'll go back to the dining room, and you send Taka there. If anyone comes, I can slip into the pantry."

"It's immoral," I protested. "It's immoral to steal your —"

"My own butler!" she broke in impatiently. "You're not usually so scrupulous, Kit. Hurry! I hear that hateful Anne Brown."

So we slid back along the hall, and I rang for Takahiro. But no one came.

"I think I ought to tell you, Bella," I said as we waited, and Bella was staring around the room — "I think you ought to know that Miss Caruthers is here."

Bella shrugged her shoulders.

"Well, thank goodness," she said, "I don't have to see her. The only pleasant thing I remember about my year of married life is that I did *not* meet Aunt Selina."

I rang again, but still there was no answer. And then it occurred to me that the stillness below stairs was almost oppressive. Bella was noticing things, too, for she began to fasten her veil again with a malicious little smile.

"One of the things I remember my late husband saying," she observed, "was that *he* could manage this house, and had done it for years, with flawless service. Stand on the bell, Kit."

I did. We stood there, with the table, just as it had been left, between us, and waited for a response. Bella was growing impatient. She raised her eyebrows (she is very handsome, Bella is) and flung out her chin as if she had begun to enjoy the horrible situation.

I thought I heard a rattle of silver from the pantry just then, and I hurried to the door in a rage. But the pantry was empty of servants and full of dishes, and all the lights were out but one, which was burning dimly. I could have sworn that I saw one of the servants duck into the stairway to the basement, but when I got there the stairs were empty, and something was burning in the kitchen below.

Bella had followed me and was peering over my shoulder curiously.

"There isn't a servant in the house," she said triumphantly. And when we went down to the kitchen, she seemed to be right. It was in disgraceful order, and one of the bottles of wine that had been banished from the dining room sat half empty on the floor.

"Drunk!" Bella said with conviction. But I didn't think so. There had not been time enough, for one thing. Suddenly I remembered the ambulance that had been the cause of Bella's appearance — for no one could believe her silly story about Takahiro. I didn't wait to voice my suspicion to her; I simply left her there, staring helplessly at the confusion, and ran upstairs again: through the dining room, past Jimmy and Aunt Selina, past Leila Mercer and Max, who were flirting on the stairs, up, up to the servants' bedrooms, and there my suspicions were verified. There was every evidence of a hasty flight; in three bedrooms five trunks stood locked and ominous, and the closets yawned with open doors, empty. Bella had been right; there was not a servant in the house.

As I emerged from the untidy emptiness of the servants' wing, I met Mr. Harbison coming out of the studio.

"I wish you would let me do some of this running about for you, Mrs. Wilson," he said gravely. "You are not well, and I can't think of anything worse for a headache. Has the butler's illness clogged the household machinery?"

"Worse," I replied, trying not to breathe in gasps. "I wouldn't be running around — like this — but there is not a servant in the house! They have gone, the entire lot."

"That's odd," he said slowly. "Gone! Are you sure?"

In reply I pointed to the servants' wing. "Trunks packed," I said tragically, "rooms empty, kitchen and pantries, full of dishes. Did you ever hear of anything like it?"

"Never," he asserted. "It makes me suspect —" What he suspected he did not say; instead he turned on his heel, without a word of explanation, and ran down the stairs. I stood staring after him, wondering if everyone in the place had gone crazy. Then I heard Betty Mercer scream and the rest talking loud and laughing, and Mr. Harbison came up the stairs again two at a time.

"How long has that Jap been ailing, Mrs. Wilson?" he asked.

"I — I don't know," I replied helplessly. "What is the trouble, anyhow?"

"I think he probably has something contagious," he said, "and it has scared the servants away. As Mr. Brown said, he looked spotty. I suggested to your husband that it might be as well to get the house emptied — in case we are correct."

"Oh, yes, by all means," I said eagerly. I couldn't get away too soon. "I'll go and get my —" Then I stopped. Why, the man wouldn't expect me to leave; I would have to play out the wretched farce to the end!

"I'll go down and see them off," I finished lamely, and we went together down the stairs.

Just for the moment I forgot Bella altogether. I found Aunt Selina bonneted and cloaked, taking a stirrup cup of Pomona for her nerves, and the rest throwing on their wraps in a hurry. Downstairs Max was telephoning for his car, which wasn't due for an hour, and Jim was walking up and down, swearing under his breath. With the prospect of getting rid of them all, and, of going home comfortably to try to forget the whole wretched affair, I cheered up quite a lot. I even played up my part of hostess, and Dallas told me, aside, that I was a brick.

Just then Jim threw open the front door.

There was a man on the top step, with his mouth full of tacks, and he was nailing something to the door, just below Jim's Florentine bronze knocker, and standing back with his head on one side to see if it was straight.

"What are you doing?" Jim demanded fiercely, but the man only drove another tack. It was Mr. Harbison who stepped outside and read the card.

It said "Smallpox."

"Smallpox," Mr. Harbison read, as if he couldn't believe it. Then he turned to us, huddled in the hall.

"It seems it wasn't measles, after all," he said cheerfully. "I move we get into Mr. Reed's automobile out there, and have a vaccination party. I suppose even you blasé society folk have not exhausted that kind of diversion."

But the man on the step spat his tacks in his hand and
spoke for the first time.

"No, you don't," he said. "Not on your life. Just step back
, please, and close the door. This house is quarantined."

Chapter V

FROM THE TREE OF LOVE

*T*here is hardly any use trying to describe what followed. Anne Brown began to cry, and talk about the children. (She went to Europe once and stayed until they all got over the whooping cough.) And Dallas said he had a pull, because his mill controlled I forget how many votes, and the thing to do was to be quiet and comfortable and we would get out in the morning. Max took it as a huge joke, and somebody found him at the telephone, calling up his club. The Mercer girls were hysterically giggling, and Aunt Selina sat on a stiff-backed chair and took aromatic spirits of ammonia. As for Jim, he had collapsed on the lowest step of the stairs, and sat there with his head in his hands. When he did look up, he didn't dare to look at me.

The Harbison man was arguing with the impassive individual on the top step outside, and I saw him get out his pocketbook and offer a crisp bundle of bills. But the man from the board of health only smiled and tacked at his offensive sign. After a while Mr. Harbison came in and closed the door, and we stared at one another.

"I know what I'm going to do," I said, swallowing a lump in my throat. "I'm going to get out through a basement window at the back. I'm going home."

"Home!" Aunt Selina gasped, jumping up and almost dropping her ammonia bottle. "My dear Bella! Home?"

Jimmy groaned at the foot of the stairs, but Anne Brown was getting over her tears and now she turned on me in a temper.

"It's all your fault," she said. "I was going to stay at home and get a little sleep —"

"Well, you can sleep now," Dallas broke in. "There'll be nothing to do but sleep."

"I think you haven't grasped the situation, Dal," I said icily. "There will be plenty to do. There isn't a servant in the house!"

"No servants!" everybody cried at once. The Mercer girls stopped giggling.

"Holy cats!" Max stopped in the act of hanging up his overcoat. "Do you mean — why, I can't shave myself! I'll cut my head off."

"You'll do more than that," I retorted grimly. "You will carry coal and tend fires and empty ash pans, and when you are not doing any of those things there will be pots and pans to wash and beds to make."

Then there *was* a row. We had worked back to the den now, and I stood in front of the fireplace and let the storm beat around me, and tried to look perfectly cold and indifferent, and not to see Mr. Harbison's shocked face. No wonder he thought them a lot of savages, browbeating their hostess the way they did.

"It's a fool thing anyhow," Max Reed wound up, "to celebrate the anniversary of a divorce — especially" Here he caught Jim's eye and stopped. But I had suddenly remembered. *Bella down in the basement!*

Could anything have been worse? And of course she would have hysteria and then turn on me and blame me for it all. It all came over me at once and overwhelmed me, while Anne was crying and saying she wouldn't cook if she starved for it, and Aunt Selina was taking off her wraps. I felt queer all over, and I sat down suddenly. Mr. Harbison was looking at me, and he brought me a glass of wine.

"It won't be so bad as you fear," he said comfortingly. "There will be no danger once we are vaccinated, and many hands make light work. They are pretty raw now, because the thing is new to them, but by morning they will be reconciled."

"It isn't the work; it is something entirely different," I said. And it was. Bella and work could hardly be spoken in the same breath.

If I had only turned her out as she deserved to be, when she first came, instead of allowing her to carry through the wretched farce about seeing Takahiro! Or if I had only run to the basement the moment the house was quarantined, and got her out the areaway or the coal hole! And now time was flying, and Aunt Selina had me by the arm, and any moment I expected Bella to pounce on us through the doorway and the whole situation to explode with a bang.

It was after eleven before they were rational enough to discuss ways and means, and, of course, the first thing suggested was that we all adjourn below stairs and clean up after dinner. I could have slain Max Reed for the notion, and the Mercer girls for taking him up.

"Of course we will," they said in a duet. "What a lark!" And they actually began to pin up their dinner gowns. It was Jim who stopped that.

"Oh, look here, you people," he objected, "I'm not going to let you do that. We'll get some servants in tomorrow. I'll go down and put out the lights. There will be enough clean dishes for breakfast."

It was lucky for me that they started a new discussion then and there about who would get the breakfast. In the midst of the excitement I slipped away to carry the news to Bella. She was where I had left her, and she had made herself a cup of tea, and was very much at home, which was natural.

"Do you know," she said ominously, "that you have been away for two hours; and that I have gone through agonies of nervousness for fear Jim Wilson would come down and think I came here to see him?"

"No one would think that, Bella," I soothed her. "Everybody knows you loathe him — Jim, too." She looked at me over the edge of her cup.

"I'll run along now," she said, "since Takahiro isn't here. And if Jim has any sense at all, he will clear out every maid in the house. I never saw such a kitchen in all my life. Well, lead the way, Kit. I suppose they are deep in bridge, or roulette, or something."

She was fixing her veil, and I saw I would have to tell her. Personally, I would much rather have told her the house was on fire.

"Wait a minute, Bella," I said. "You see, something queer has happened. You know this is the anniversary — well, you know what it is — and Jim was awfully glum. So we thought we would come —"

"What are you driving at?" she demanded. "You are sea-green, Kit. What's the matter? You needn't think I mind because Jim has a jollification to celebrate his divorce."

"It — it was Takahiro — in the ambulance," I blurted. "Smallpox. We — Bella, we are shut in, quarantined."

She didn't faint. She just sat down and stared at me, and I stared back at her. Then a miserable alarm clock on the table suddenly went off like an explosion, and Bella began to laugh. I knew what that was — hysteria. She always had attacks like that when things went wrong. I was quite despairing by that time; I hoped they would all hear her and come downstairs and take her up and put her to bed like a Christian, so she could giggle her soul out. But after a bit she quieted down and began to cry softly, and I knew the worst was over. I gave her a shake, and she was so angry that she got over it altogether.

"Kit, you are horrid," she choked. "Don't you see what a position I am in? I am not going upstairs to face Anne and the rest of them. You can just put me in the coal cellar."

"Isn't there a window you could get through?" I asked desperately. "Locking the door doesn't shut up a whole house."

Bella's courage revived at that, and she said yes, there were windows, plenty of them, only she didn't see how she could get out. And I said she would *have* to get out, because I was playing Bella in the performance, and I didn't care to have an understudy. Then the situation dawned on her, and she sat down and laughed herself weak in the knees. Of course she wanted to stay, then, and see the fun out. But I was firm; she would have to go, and I told her so. Things were complicated enough without her.

Well, we looked funny, no doubt, Bella in a Russian pony automobile coat over the black satin she had worn at the Clevelands' dinner, and I in cream lace, the skirt gathered up from the kitchen floor, with Bella's ermine pelerine around my bare shoulders, and dishes and overturned chairs everywhere.

Bella knew more about the lower regions of her ex-home than I would have thought. She opened a door in a corner and led the way through a narrow hall past the refrigerating room, to a huge, cemented cellar, with a furnace in the center, and a half-dozen electric lights making it really brilliant.

"Get a chair," Bella said over her shoulder, excitedly. "I can get out easily here, through the coal hole. Imagine my —"

But it was my turn to grip Bella. From behind the furnace were coming the most terrible sounds, rasping noises that fairly frayed the silk of my nerves. We stood petrified for an instant. Then Bella laughed. "They are not all gone,:" she said carefully. "Some one is asleep there."

We tiptoed to where we could see around the furnace, and, sure enough, some one *was* asleep there. Only, it was not one of the servants; it was a portly policeman, with a newspaper and an empty plate on the floor on one side, and a champagne bottle on the other. He had slid down in his chair, with his chin on his brass buttons, and his helmet had rolled a dozen feet away. Bella had to clap her hand over her mouth.

"Fairly caught!" she whispered. "Sartor Resartus, the arrester arrested. Oh, Jim and his flawless service!"

But after we got over our surprise, we saw the situation was serious. The policeman was threatening to awaken. Once he stopped snoring to yawn noisily, and we beat a hasty retreat. Bella switched off the lights in a hurry and locked the door behind us. We hardly breathed until we were back in the kitchen again, and everything quiet. And then Jimmy called my name from up above somewheres.

"I am going to call him down, Bella," I said firmly. "Let him help you out. I'm sure I don't see why I should have all this when the two of you —"

"Oh, no, no! Surely, Kit, you wouldn't be so cruel!" she whispered pleadingly. "You know what he would think. He — oh, Kit, let them all get settled for the night, and then come down, like a dear, and help me out. I know loads of ways — honestly I do."

"If I leave you here," I debated, "what about the policeman?"

"Never mind him" — frantically. "Listen! There's Jim up in the pantry. Run, for the sake of Heaven!"

So — I ran. At the top of the stairs I met Jimmy, very crumpled as to shirt-front and dejected as to face.

"I've been hunting everywhere for you," he said dismally. "I thought you had added to the general merriment by falling downstairs and breaking your neck."

I went past him with my chin up. Now that I had time to think about it, I was furiously angry with him.

"Kit!" he called after me appealingly, but I would not hear. Then he adopted different tactics. He took advantage of my catching my foot in the lace of my gown to pass me, and to stand with his back against the door.

"You're not going until you hear me, Kit," he declared miserably. "In the first place, for all you are down on me, is it my fault? Honestly, now *is it my fault?*"

I refused to speak.

"I was coming home to be miserable alone," he went on, "and — oh, I know you meant well, Kit; but *you* asked all these crazy people here."

"Perhaps you will give me credit for some things," I said wearily. "I did *not* give Takahiro smallpox, for instance, and — if you will permit me to mention the fact — Aunt Selina is not *my* Aunt Selina."

"That's what I wanted to speak to you about," Jimmy went on wretchedly, trying not to look at me. "You see, when they were rowing so about who would get the breakfast — I never saw such a lot of people; half of them never touch breakfast, but of course now they want all kinds of things — when they were talking, Aunt Selina said she knew *you* would get it, being the hostess, and responsible, besides knowing where things are kept." He had fixed his eyes on the orchids, and he looked shrunken, actually shrunken. "I thought," he finished, "you might give me a few pointers now, and I could come down in the morning, and — and fuss up something, coffee and so on. I would say you did it! Oh, hang it all, Kit, why don't you say something?"

"What do you want me to say?" I demanded. "That I love to cook, and of course I'll fix trays and carry them up in the morning to Anne Brown and Leila Mercer and the rest; and that I will have the shaving water ready —"

"I know what I'm going to do," Jimmy said, with a sudden resolution. "Aunt Selina and her money can go to blazes. I am going right upstairs and tell her the truth, tell her who you are, what I am, and all the rest of it." He opened the door.

"You'll do nothing of the kind," I gasped, catching him in time. "Don't you dare, Jimmy Wilson! Why, what would they think of me? After letting her call me Bella, and him — Jim, if Mr. Harbison ever learns the truth — I — I will take poison. If we are going to be shut up here together, we will have to carry it on. I couldn't stand the disgrace."

In spite of an heroic effort, Jim looked relieved. "They have been hunting for the linen closet," he said, more cheerfully, "and there will be room enough, I think. Harbison and I will hang out in the studio; there are two couches there. I'm afraid you'll have to take Aunt Selina, Kit."

"Certainly," I said coldly. That was the way it was all along. Whenever there was something to do that no one else would undertake — any unpleasant responsibility — that entire mongrel household turned with one gesture and pointed its finger at me! Well, it is over now, and I ought not to be bitter, considering everything.

It was quite characteristic of that memorable evening (that is quite novelesque, I think) that my interview with Jimmy should have a sensational ending. He was terribly down, of course, and as I was trying to pass him to get to the door, he caught my hand.

"You're a girl in a thousand, Kit," he said forlornly. "If I were not so damnably, hopelessly, idiotically in love with — somebody else, I should be crazy about you."

"Don't be maudlin," I retorted. "Would you mind letting my hand go?" I felt sure Bella could hear.

"Oh, come now, Kit," he implored, "we've always got along so well. It's a shame to let a thing like this make us bad friends. Aren't you ever going to forgive me?"

"Never," I said promptly. "When I once get away, I don't want ever to see you again. I was never so humiliated in my life. I loathe you!"

Then I turned around, and, of course, there was Aunt Selina with her eyes protruding until you could have knocked them off with a stick, and beside her, very red and uncomfortable, Mr. Harbison!

"Bella!" she said in a shocked voice, "is that the way you speak to your husband! It is high time I came here, I think, and took a hand in this affair."

"Oh, never mind, Aunt Selina," Jim said, with a sheepish grin. "Kit — Bella is tired and nervous. This is a h—— deuce of a situation. No — er — servants, and all that."

But Aunt Selina did mind, and showed it. She pulled the unlucky Harbison man through the door and closed it, and then stood glaring at both of us.

"Every little quarrel is an apple knocked from the tree of love," she announced oratorically.

"This was a very little quarrel," Jim said, edging toward the door; "a — a green apple, Aunt Selina, a colicky little green apple." But she was not to be diverted.

"Bella," she said severely, "you said you loathed him. You didn't mean that."

"But I do!" I cried hysterically. "There isn't any word to tell how I — how I detest him."

Then I swept past them all and flew to Bella's dressing room and locked myself in. Aunt Selina knocked until she was tired, then gave up and went to bed.

That was the night Anne Brown's pearl collar was stolen!

Chapter VI
A MIGHTY POOR JOKE

Of course, one knows that there are people who in a different grade of society would be shoplifters and pickpockets. When they are restrained by obligation or environment they become a little overkeen at bridge, or take the wrong sables, or stuff a gold-backed brush into a muff at a reception. You remember the ivory dressing set that Theodora Bucknell had, fastened with fine gold chains? And the sensation it caused at the Bucknell cotillion when Mrs. Van Zire went sweeping to her carriage with two feet of gold chain hanging from the front of her wrap?

But Anne's pearl collar was different. In the first place, instead of three or four hundred people, the suspicion had to be divided among ten. And of those ten, at least eight of us were friends, and the other two had been vouched for by the Browns and Jimmy. It was a horrible mix-up. For the necklace was gone — there couldn't be any doubt of that — and although, as Dallas said, it couldn't get out of the house, still, there were plenty of places to hide the thing.

The worst of our trouble really originated with Max Reed, after all. For it was Max who made the silly wager over the telephone, with Dick Bagley. He bet five hundred even that one of us, at least, would break quarantine within the next twenty-four hours, and, of course, that settled it. Dick told it around the club as a joke, and a man who owns a newspaper heard him and called up the paper. Then the paper called up the health office, after setting up a flaming scare-head, "Will

Money Free Them? Board of Health versus Millionaire."

It was almost three when the house settled down — nobody had any night clothes, although finally, through Dallas, who gave them to Anne, who gave them to the rest, we got some things of Jimmy's — and I was still dressed. The house was perfectly quiet, and, after listening carefully, I went slowly down the stairs. There was a light in the hall, and another back in the dining room, and I got along without any trouble. But the pantry, where the stairs led down, was dark, and the wretched swinging door would not stay open.

I caught my skirt in the door as I went through, and I had to stop to loosen it. And in that awful minute I heard some one breathing just beside me. I had stooped to my gown, and I turned my head without straightening — I couldn't have raised myself to an erect posture, for my knees were giving way under me — and just at my feet lay the still glowing end of a match!

I had to swallow twice before I could speak. Then I said sharply:

"Who's there?"

The man was so close it is a wonder I had not walked into him; his voice was right at my ear.

"I am sorry I startled you," he said quietly. "I was afraid to speak suddenly, or move, for fear I would do — what I have done."

It was Mr. Harbison.

"I — I thought you were — it is very late," I managed to say, with dry lips. "Do you know where the electric switch is?"

"Mrs. Wilson!" It was clear he had not known me before. "Why, no; don't you?"

"I am all confused," I muttered, and beat a retreat into the dining room. There, in the friendly light, we could at least see each other, and I think he was as much impressed by the fact that I had not undressed as I was by the fact that he *had*, partly. He wore a hideous dressing gown of Jimmy's, much too small, and his hair, parted and plastered down in the early evening, stood up in a sort of brown brush all over his head. He was trying to flatten it with his hands.

"It must be three o'clock," he said, with polite surprise, "and the house is like a barn. You ought not to be running around with your arms uncovered, Mrs. Wilson. Surely you could have called some of us."

"I didn't wish to disturb anyone," I said, with distinct truth.

"I suppose you are like me," he said. "The novelty of the situation — and everything. I got to thinking things over, and then I realized the studio was getting cold, so I thought I would come down and take a look at the furnace. I didn't suppose anyone else would think of it. But I lost myself in that pantry, stumbled against a half-open drawer, and nearly went down the dumb-waiter." And, as if in judgment on me, at that instant came two rather terrific thumps from somewhere below, and inarticulate words, shouted rather than spoken. It was uncanny, of course, coming as it did through the register at our feet. Mr. Harbison looked startled.

"Oh, by the way," I said, as carelessly as I could. "In the excitement, I forgot to mention it. There is a policeman asleep in the furnace room. I — I suppose we will have to keep him now," I finished as airily as possible.

"Oh, a policeman — in the cellar," he repeated, staring at me, and he moved toward the pantry door.

"You needn't go down," I said feverishly, with visions of Bella Knowles sitting on the kitchen table, surrounded by soiled dishes and all the cheerless aftermath of a dinner party. "Please don't go down. I — it's one of my rules — never to let a stranger go down to the kitchen. I — I'm peculiar — that way — and besides, it's — it's mussy."

Bang! Crash! through the register pipe, and some language quite articulate. Then silence.

"Look here, Mrs. Wilson," he said resolutely. "What do I care about the kitchen? I'm going down and arrest that policeman for disturbing the peace. He will have the pipes down."

"You must not go," I said with desperate firmness. "He — he is probably in a very dangerous state just now. We — I — locked him in."

The Harbison man grinned and then became serious.

"Why don't you tell me the whole thing?" he demanded. "You've been in trouble all evening, and — you can trust me, you know, because I am a stranger; because the minute this crazy quarantine is raised I am off to the Argentine Republic," (perhaps he said Chili) "and because I don't know anything at all about you. You see, I have to believe what you tell me, having no personal knowledge of any of you to go on. Now tell me — whom have you hidden in the cellar, besides the policeman?"

There was no use trying to deceive him; he was looking straight into my eyes. So I decided to make the best of a bad thing. Anyhow, it was going to require strength to get Bella through the coal hole with one arm and restrain the policeman with the other.

"Come," I said, making a sudden resolution, and led the way down the stairs.

He said nothing when he saw Bella, for which I was grateful. She was sitting at the table, with her arms in front of her, and her head buried in them. And then I saw she was asleep. Her hat and veil laid beside her, and she had taken off her coat and draped it around her. She had rummaged out a cold pheasant and some salad, and had evidently had a little supper. Supper and a nap, while I worried myself gray-headed about her!

"She — she came in unexpectedly — something about the butler," I explained under my breath. "And — she doesn't want to stay. She is on bad terms with — with some of the people upstairs. You can see how impossible the situation is."

"I doubt if we can get her out," he said, as if the situation were quite ordinary. "However, we can try. She seems very comfortable. It's a pity to rouse her."

Here the prisoner in the furnace room broke out afresh. It sounded as though he had taken a lump of coal and was attacking the lock. Mr. Harbison followed the noise, and I could hear him arguing, not gently.

"Another sound," he finished, "and you won't get out of here at all, unless you crawl up the furnace pipe!"

When he came back, Bella was rousing. She lifted her head with her eyes shut and then opened them one at a time, blinked, and sat up. She didn't see him at first.

"You wretch!" she said ungratefully, after she had yawned. "Do you know what time it is? And that —" Then she saw Mr. Harbison and sat staring at him.

"This is Mr. Harbison," I said to her hastily. "He — he came with Anne and Dal and — he is shut in, too."

By that time Bella had seen how handsome he was, and she took a hair pin out of her mouth, and arched her eyebrows, which was always Bella's best pose.

"I am Miss Knowles," she said sweetly (of course, the court had given her back her name), "and I stopped in tonight, thinking the house was empty, to see about a — a butler. Unfortunately, the house was quarantined just at that time, and — here I am. Surely there can not be any harm in helping me to get out?" (Pleading tone.) "I have not been exposed to any contagion, and in the exhausted state of my health the confinement would be positively dangerous."

She rolled her eyes at him, and I could see she was making an impression. Of course she was free. She had a perfect right to marry again, but I will say this: Bella is a lot better looking by electric light than she is the next morning.

The upshot of it was that the gentleman who built bridges and looked down on society from a lofty, lonely pinnacle agreed to help one of the most gleaming members of the aforesaid society to outwit the law.

It took about fifteen minutes to quiet the policeman. Nobody ever knew what Mr. Harbison did to him, but for twenty-four hours he was quite tractable. He changed after that, but that comes later in the story. Anyhow, the Harbison man went upstairs and came down with a Baghdad curtain and a cushion to match, and took them into the furnace room, and came out and locked the door behind him, and then we were ready for Bella's escape.

But there were four special officers and three reporters watching the house, as a result of Max Reed's idiocy. Once, after trying all the other windows and finding them guarded, we discovered a little bit of a hole in an out-of-the-way corner that looked like a ventilator and was covered with a heavy wire screen. No prisoners ever dug their way out of a dungeon with more energy than that with which we attached that screen, hacking at it with kitchen knives, whispering like conspirators, being scratched with the ragged edges of the wire, frozen with the cold air one minute and boiling with excitement the next. And when the wire was cut, and Bella had rolled her coat up and thrust it through and was standing on a chair ready to follow, something outside that had looked like a barrel moved, and said, "Oh, I wouldn't do that if I were you. It would be certain to be undignified, and probably it would be unpleasant — later."

We coaxed and pleaded and tried to bribe, and that happened, as it turned out, to be one of the worst things we had to endure. For the whole conversation came out the next afternoon in the paper, with the most awful drawings, and the reporter said it was the flashing of the jewels we wore that first attracted his attention. And that brings me back to the robbery.

For when we had crept back to the kitchen, and Bella was fumbling for her handkerchief to cry into and the Harbison man was trying to apologize for the language he had used to the reporter, and I was on the verge of a nervous chill — well, it was then that Bella forgot all about crying and jumped and held out her arm.

"My diamond bracelet!" she screeched. "Look, I've lost it."

Well, we went over every inch of that basement, until I knew every crack in the flooring, every spot on the cement. And Bella was nasty, and said that she had never seen that part of the house in such condition, and that if I had acted like a sane person and put her out, when she had no business there at all, she would have had her freedom and her bracelet, and that if we were playing a joke on her (as if we felt like joking!) we would please give her the bracelet and let her go and die in a corner; she felt very queer.

At half-past four o'clock we gave up.

"It's gone," I said. "I don't believe you wore it here. No one could have taken it. There wasn't a soul in this part of the house, except the policeman and he's locked in."

At five o'clock we put her to sleep in the den. She was in a fearful temper, and I was glad enough to be able to shut the door on her. Tom Harbison — that was his name — helped me to creep upstairs, and wanted to get me a glass of ale to make me sleep. But I said it would be of no use, as I had to get up and get the breakfast. The last thing he said was that the policeman seemed above the average in intelligence, and perhaps we could train him to do plain cooking and dishwashing.

I did not go to sleep at once. I lay on the chintz-covered divan in Bella's dressing room and stared at the picture of her with the violets underneath. I couldn't see what there was about Bella to inspire such undying devotion, but I had to admit that she had looked handsome that night, and that the Harbison man had certainly been impressed.

At seven o'clock Jimmy Wilson pounded at my door, and I could have choked him joyfully. I dragged myself to the door and opened it, and then I heard excited voices. Everybody seemed to be up but Aunt Selina, and they were all talking at once.

Anne Brown was in the corner of the group, waving her hands, while Dallas was trying to hook the back of her gown with one hand and hold a blanket around himself with the other. No one was dressed except Anne, and she had been up for an hour, looking in shoes and under the corners of rugs and around the bed clothing for her jeweled collar. When she saw me she began all over again.

"I had it on when I went into my room," she declared, "and I put it on the dressing table when I undressed. I meant to put it under my pillow, but I forgot. And I didn't sleep well; I was awake half the night. Wasn't I, Dal? Then, when the clock downstairs in the hall was chiming five, something roused me, and I sat up in bed. It was still dark, but I pinched Dal and said there was somebody in the room. You remember that, don't you, Dal?"

"I thought you had nightmare,:" he said sheepishly.

"I lay still for ages, it seemed to me, and then — the door into the hall closed. I heard the catch click. I turned on the light over the bed then, and the room was empty. I thought of my collar, and although it seemed ridiculous, with the house sealed as it is, and all of us friends for years — well, I got up and looked, and it was gone!"

No one spoke for an instant. It *was* a queer situation, for the collar was gone; Anne's red eyes showed it was true. And there we stood, every one of us a miserable picture of guilt, and tried to look innocent and debonair and unsuspicious. Finally Jim held up his hand and signified that he wanted to say something.

"It's like this," he said, "until this thing is cleared up, for Heaven's sake, let's try to be sane! If every fellow thinks the other fellow did it, this house will be a nice little hell to live in. And if anybody" — here he glared around — "if anybody has got funny and is hiding those jewels, I want to say that he'd better speak up now. Later, it won't be so easy for him. It's a mighty poor joke."

But nobody spoke.

Chapter VII
WE MAKE AN OMELET

*I*t was Betty Mercer who said she was hungry, and got us switched from the delicate subject of which was the thief to the quite as pressing subject of which was to be cook. Aunt Selina had slept quietly through the whole thing — we learned afterward that she customarily slept on her left side, which was on her good ear. We gathered in the Dallas Browns' room, and Jimmy proposed a plan.

"We can have anything sent in that we want," he suggested speciously, "and if Dal doesn't make good with the city fathers, you girls can get some clothes anyhow. Then, we can have dinner sent from one of the hotels."

"Why not all the meals?" Max suggested. "I hope you're not going to be small about things, Jimmy."

"It ought to be easy," Jim persisted, ignoring the remark, "for nine reasonably intelligent people to boil eggs and make coffee, which is all we need for breakfast, with some fruit."

"Nine of us!" Dallas said wickedly, looking at Tom Harbison, who was out of earshot, "Why nine of us? I thought Kit here, otherwise known as Bella, was going to show off her housewifely skill."

It ended, however, with Mr. Harbison writing out a lot of slips, cook, scullery-maid, chamber-maid, parlor-maid, furnace-man, and butler, and as that left two people over — we didn't count Aunt Selina — he added another furnace-man and a trained nurse. Betty Mercer drew the trained nurse slip, and, of course, she was delighted. It seems funny now to look

back and think what a dreadful time she really had, for Aunt
Selina took the grippe, you know, that very day.

It was fate that I should go back to that awful kitchen, for
of course my slip said "cook." Mr. Harbison was butler, and
Max and Dal got the furnace, although neither of them had
ever been nearer to a bucket of coal than the coupons on
mining stock. Anne got the bedrooms, and Leila was parlor-
maid. It was Jimmy who got the scullery work, but he was
quite crushed by this time, and did not protest at all.

Max was in a very bad temper; I suppose he had not had
enough sleep — no one had. But he came over while the lottery
was going on and stood over me and demanded unpleasantly,
in a whisper, that I stop masquerading as another man's wife
and generally making a fool of myself — which is the way he
put it. And I knew in my heart that he was right, and I hated
him for it.

"Why don't you go and tell him — them?" I asked nastily.
No one was paying any attention to us. "Tell them that, to
be obliging, I have nearly drowned in a sea of lies; tell them
that I am not only not married, but that I never intend to
marry; tell them that we are a lot of idiots with nothing better
to do than to trifle with strangers within our gates, people
who build — I mean, people that are worth two to our one!
Run and tell them."

He looked at me for a minute, then he turned on his heel
and left me. It looked as though Max might be going to be
difficult.

While I was improvising an apron out of a towel, and Anne
was pinning a sheet into a kimono, so she could take off her
dinner gown and still be proper, Dallas harked back to the
robbery.

"Ann put the collar on the table there," he said. "There's
no mistake about that. I watched her do it, for I remember
thinking it was the sole reminder I had that Consolidated
Traction ever went above thirty-nine."

Max was looking around the room, examining the window
locks and whistling between his teeth. He was in disgrace with
everyone, for by that time it was light enough to see three
reporters with cameras across the street waiting for enough
sun to snap the house, and everybody knew that it was Max

and his idiotic wager that had done it. He had made two or three conciliatory remarks, but no one would speak to him. His antics were so queer, however, that we were all watching him, and when he had felt over the rug with his hands, and raised the edges, and tried to lift out the chair seats, and had shaken out Dal's shoes (he said people often hid things and then forgot about it), he made a proposition.

"If you will take that infernal furnace from around my neck, I'll undertake either to find the jewels or to show up the thief," he said quietly. And of course, with all the people in the house under suspicion, everyone had to hail the suggestion with joy, and to offer his assistance, and Jimmy had to take Max's share of the furnace. So they took the scullery slip downstairs to the policeman, and gave Jim Max's share of the furnace. (Yes, I had broken the policeman to them gently. Of course, Anne said at once that he was the thief, but they found him tucked in and sound asleep with his back against the furnace.)

"In the first place," Max said, standing importantly in the middle of the room, "we retired between two and three — nearer three. So the theft occurred between three and five, when Anne woke up. Was your door locked, Dal?"

"No. The door into the hall was, but the door into the dressing room was open, and we found the door from there into the hall open this morning."

"From three until five," Max repeated. "Was anyone out of his room during that time?"

"I was," said Tom Harbison promptly, from the foot of the bed. "I was prowling all around somewhere about four, search-ing" — he glanced at me — "for a drink of water. But as I don't know a pearl from a glass bead, I hope you exonerate me."

Everybody laughed and said, "Of course," and "Sure, old man," and changed the subject quickly.

While that excitement was on, I got Jim to one side and told him about Bella. His good-natured face was radiant at first.

"I suppose she *did* come to see Takahiro, eh, Kit?" he asked delicately. "She didn't say anything about me?"

"Nothing good. She said the house was in a disgraceful condition," I said heartlessly. "And her diamond bracelet was stolen while she took a nap on the kitchen table" — he groaned — "and — oh, Jim, you are such a goose! If I could only manage my own affairs the way I could my friends'! She's too sure of you, Jimmy. She knows you adore her, and — how brutal could you be, Jim?"

"Fair," he said. "I may have undiscovered depths of brutality that I have never had occasion to use. However, I might try. Why?"

"Listen, Jim," I urged. "It was always Bella who did things here; she managed the house, she tyrannized over her friends, and she bullied you. Yes, she did. Now she's here, without your invitation, and she has to stay. It's your turn to bully, to dictate terms, to be coldly civil or politely rude. Make her furious at you. If she is jealous, so much the better."

"How far would you sacrifice yourself on the altar of friendship?" he asked.

"You may pay me all the attention you like, in public," I replied, and after we shook hands we went together to Bella.

There was an ominous pause when we went into the den. Bella was sitting by the register, with her furs on, and after one glance over her shoulder at us, she looked away again without speaking.

"Bella," Jim said appealingly. And then I pinched his arm, and he drew himself up and looked properly outraged.

"Bella," he said, coldly this time, "I can't imagine why you have put yourself in this ridiculous position, but since you have —"

She turned on him in a fury.

"Put *myself* in this position!"

She was frantic. "It's a plot, a wretched trick of yours, this quarantine, to keep me here."

Jim gasped, but I gave him a warning glance, and he swallowed hard.

"On the contrary," he said, with maddening quiet, "I would be the last person in the world to wish to perpetuate an indiscretion of yours. For it was hardly discreet, was it, to visit a bachelor establishment alone at ten o'clock at night? As far as my plotting to keep you here is concerned, I assure you that nothing could be further from my mind. Our paths were to be two parallel lines that never touch." He looked at me for approval, and Bella was choking.

"You are worse that I ever thought you," she stormed. "I thought you were only a — a fool. Now I know you — for a brute!"

Well, it ended by Jim's graciously permitting Bella to remain — there being nothing else to do — and by his magnanimously agreeing to keep her real identity from Aunt Selina and Mr. Harbison, and to break the news of her presence to Anne and the rest. It created a sensation beside which Anne's pearls faded away, although they came to the front again soon enough.

Jim broke the news at once, gathering everybody but Harbison and Aunt Selina in the upper hall. He was palpitatingly nervous, but he tried to carry it off with a high hand.

"It's unfortunate," he said, looking around the circle of faces, each one frozen with amazement, and just a suspicion, perhaps of incredulity. "It's particularly unfortunate for her. You all know how high-strung she is, and if the papers should get hold of it — well, we'll all have to make it as easy as we can for her."

With Jim's eyes on them, they all swallowed the butler story without a gulp. But Anne was indignant.

"It's like Bella," she snapped. "Well, she has made her bed and she can lie on it. I'm sure I shan't make it for her. But if you want to know my opinion, Mr. Harbison may be a fool, but you can't ram two Bellas, both *nee* Knowles, down Miss Caruthers' throat with a stick."

We had not thought of that before and everyone looked blank. Finally, however, Jim said Bella's middle name was Constantia, and we decided to call her that. But it turned out afterward that nobody could remember it in a hurry, and generally when we wanted to attract her attention, we walked across the room and touched her on the shoulder. It was quicker and safer.

The name decided, we went downstairs in a line to welcome Bella, to try to make her feel at home, and to forget her deplorable situation. Leila had worked herself into a really sympathetic frame of mind.

"Poor dear," she said, on the way down. "Now don't grin, anybody, just be cordial and glad to see her. I hope she doesn't cry; you know the spells she takes."

We stopped outside the door, and everybody tried to look cheerful and sympathetic, and not grinny — which was as hard as looking as if we had had a cup of tea — and then Jim threw the door open and we filed in.

Bella was comfortably reading by the fire. She had her feet up on a stool and a pillow behind her head. She did not even look at us for a minute; then she merely glanced up as she turned a page.

"Dear me," she said mockingly, "what a lot of frumps you all are! I had hoped it was some one with my breakfast."

Then she went on reading. As Leila said afterward, that kind of person *ought* to be divorced.

Aunt Selina came down just then and I left everybody trying to explain Bella's presence to her, and fled to the kitchen. The Harbison man appeared while I was sitting hopelessly in front of the gas range, and showed me about it.

"I don't know that I ever saw one," he said cheerfully, "but I know the theory. Likewise, by the same token, this tea kettle, set on the flame, will boil. That is not theory, however, that is early knowledge. 'Polly, put the kettle on; we'll all take tea.' Look at that, Mrs. Wilson. I didn't fight bacilli with boiled water at Chickamauga for nothing."

And then he let out the policeman and brought him into the kitchen. He was a large man, and his face was a curious mixture of amazement, alarm and dignity. No doubt we did look queer, still in parts of our evening clothes and I in the white silk and lace petticoat that belonged under my gown, with a yellow and black pajama coat of Jimmy's as a sort of breakfast jacket.

"This is Officer Flannigan," Mr. Harbison said. "I explained our unfortunate position earlier in the morning, and he is prepared to accept our hospitality. Flannigan, every person in this house has got to work, as I also explained to you. You are appointed dishwasher and scullery maid."

The policeman looked dazed. Then, slowly, like dawn over a sleeping lake, a light of comprehension grew in his face.

"Sure," he said, laying his helmet on the table. "I'll be glad to be doing anything I can to help. Me and Mrs. Wilson — we used to be friends. It's many the time I've opened the carriage door for her, and she with her head in the air, and for all that, the pleasant smile. When anyone around her was having a party and wanted a special officer, it was Mrs. Wilson that always said, Get Flannigan, Officer Timothy Flannigan. He's your man.'"

My heart had been going lower and lower. So he knew Bella, and he knew I was not Bella, although he had not grasped the fact that I was usurping her place. The odious Harbison man sat on the table and swung his feet.

"I wonder if you know," he said, looking around him, "how good it is to see a white woman so perfectly at home in a civilized kitchen again, after two years of food cooked by a filthy Indian squaw over a portable sheet-iron stove!"

So perfectly at home? I stood in the middle of the room and stared around at the copper things hanging up and the rows of blue and white crockery, and the dozens and hundreds of complicated-looking utensils, whose names I had never even heard, and I was dazed. I tried with some show of authority to instruct Flannigan about gathering up the soiled things, and, after listening in puzzled silence for a minute, he stripped off his blue coat with a tolerant smile.

"Lave 'em to me, miss," he said. The "miss" passed unnoticed. "I mayn't give 'em a Turkish bath, which is what you are describin', but I'll get the grease off all right. I always clean up while the missus is in bed with a young un."

He rolled up his sleeves, found a brown checked gingham apron behind the door, and tied it around his neck with the ease of practice. Then he cleared off the plates, eating what appealed to him as he did so, and stopping now and again for a deep-throated chuckle.

"I'm thinkin'," he said once, stopping with a dish in the air, "what a deuce of a noise there will be when the vaccination doctor comes around this mornin'. In a week every one of us will be nursin' a sore arm or walkin' on one leg, beggin' your pardon, miss. The last time the force was vaccinated, I asked to be done behind me ear; I needed me legs and I needed me arms, but didn't need me head much!"

He threw his head back and laughed. Mr. Harbison laughed. Oh, we were very cheerful! And that awful stove stared at me, and the kettle began to hum, and Aunt Selina sent down word that she was not well, and would like some omelet on her tray. Omelet!

I knew that it was made of eggs, but that was the extent of my knowledge. I muttered an excuse and ran upstairs to Anne, but she was still sniffling over her necklace, and said she didn't know anything about omelets and didn't care. Food would choke her. Neither of the Mercer girls knew either, and Bella, who was still reading in the den, absolutely declined to help.

"I don't know, and I wouldn't tell you if I did. You can get yourself out, as you got yourself in," she said nastily. "The simplest thing, if you don't mind my suggesting it, is to poison the coffee and kill the lot of us. Only, if you decide to do it, let me know; I want to live just long enough to see Jimmy Wilson *writhe!*"

Bella is the kind of person who gets on one's nerves. She finds a grievance and hugs it; she does ridiculous things and blames other people. And she flirts.

I went downstairs despondently, and found that Mr. Harbison had discovered some eggs and was standing helplessly staring at them.

"Omelet — eggs. Eggs — omelet. That's the extent of my knowledge," he said, when I entered. "You'll have to come to my assistance."

It was then that I saw the cook book. It was lying on a shelf beside the clock, and while Mr. Harbison had his back turned I got it down. It was quite clear that the domestic type of woman was his ideal, and I did not care to outrage his belief in me. So I took the cook book into the pantry and read the recipe over three times. When I came back I knew it by heart, although I did not understand it.

"I will tell you how," I said with a great deal of dignity, "and since you want to help, you may make it yourself."

He was delighted.

"Fine!" he said. "Suppose you give me the idea first. Then we'll go over it slowly, bit by bit. We'll make a big fluffy omelet, and if the others aren't around, we'll eat it ourselves."

"Well," I said, trying to remember exactly, "you take two eggs —"

"Two!" he repeated. "Two eggs for ten people!"

"Don't interrupt me," I said irritably. "If — if two isn't enough we can make several omelets, one after the other."

He looked at me with admiration.

"Who else but you would have thought of that!" he remarked. "Well, here are two eggs. What next?"

"Separate them," I said easily. No, I didn't know what it meant. I hoped he would; I said it as casually as I could, and I did not look at him. I knew he was staring at me, puzzled.

"Separate them!" he said. "Why, they aren't fastened together!" Then he laughed. "Oh, yes, of course!" When I looked he had put one at each end of the table. "Afraid they'll quarrel, I suppose," he said. "Well, now they're separated."

"Then beat."

"First separate, then beat!" he repeated. "The author of that cook book must have had a mean disposition. What's next? Hang them?" He looked up at me with his boyish smile.

"Separate and beat," I repeated. If I lost a word of that recipe I was gone. It was like saying the alphabet; I had to go to the beginning every time mentally.

"Well," he reflected, "you can't beat an egg, no matter how cruel you may be, unless you break it first." He picked up an egg and looked at it. "Separate!" he reflected. "Ah — the white from the — whatever you cooking experts call it — the yellow part."

"Exactly!" I exclaimed, light breaking on me. "Of course. I *knew* you would find it out." Then back to the recipe — "beat until well mixed; then fold in the whites."

"Fold?" he questioned. "It looks pretty thin to fold, doesn't it? I — upon my word, I never heard of folding an egg. Are you — but of course you know. Please come and show me how."

"Just fold them in," I said desperately. "It isn't difficult." And because I was so transparent a fraud and knew he must find me out then, I said something about butter, and went into the pantry. That's the trouble with a lie; somebody asks you to tell one as a favor to somebody else, and the first thing you know, you are having to tell a thousand, and trying to remember the ones you have told so you won't contradict yourself, and the very person you have tried to help turns on you and reproaches you for being untruthful! I leaned my

elbows despondently on the shelf of the kitchen pantry, with
the feet of a guard visible through the high window over my
head, and waited for Mr. Harbison to come in and demand
that I fold a raw egg, and discover that I didn't know anything
about cooking, and was just as useless as all the others.

He came. He held the bowl out to me and waved a fork in
triumph.

"I have solved it," he said. "Or, rather, Flannigan and I
have solved it. The mixture awaits the magic touch of the
cook."

I honestly thought I could do the rest. It was only to be
put in a pan and browned, and then in the oven three
minutes. And I did it properly, but for two things: I should
have greased the pan (but this was the book's fault; it didn't
say) and I should have lighted the oven. The latter, however,
was Mr. Harbison's fault as much as mine, and I had wit
enough to lay it to absent-mindedness on the part of both of
us.

After that, Aunt Selina or no Aunt Selina, we decided to
have boiled eggs, and Mr. Harbison knew how to cook them.
He put them in the tea kettle and then went to look at the
furnace. And Officer Timothy Flannigan ground the coffee
and gave his opinion of the board of health in no stinted
terms. As for me, I burned my fingers and the toast, and felt
myself growing hot and cold, for I was going to be found out
as soon as Flannigan grasped the situation.

Then, of course, I did the thing that caused me so much
trouble later. I put down the toaster — at least the Harbison
man said it was a toaster — and went over and stood in front
of the policeman.

"I don't suppose you will understand — exactly," I said,
"but — but if anything occurs to — to make you think I am
not — that things are not what they seem to be — I mean, what
I say they are — you will understand that it is a joke, won't
you? A joke, you know."

Yes, that was what I said. I know it sounds like a raving
delirium, but when Max came down and squizzled some
bacon, as he said, and told Flannigan about the robbery, and
how, whether it was a joke or deadly earnest, somebody in
the house had taken Anne's pearls, that wretched policeman

winked at me solemnly over Max's shoulder. Oh, it was awful!

And, to add to my discomfort, the most unpleasant ideas *would* obtrude themselves. *What* was Mr. Harbison doing on the first floor of the house that night? Ice water, he had said. But there had been plenty of water in the studio! And he had told me it was the furnace.

Mr. Harbison came back in a half hour, and I remembered the eggs. We fished them out of the tea kettle, and they were perfectly hard, but we ate them.

The doctor from the board of health came that morning and vaccinated us. There was a great deal of excitement, and Aunt Selina was done on the arm. As she did not affect evening clothes this was entirely natural, but later on in the week, when the wretched things began to take, nobody dared to limp, and Leila made a terrible break by wearing a bandage on her left arm, after telling Aunt Selina that she had been vaccinated on the right.

Chapter VIII
CORRESPONDENTS' DEPARTMENT

*T*he following letters were found in the house post box after the lifting of the quarantine, and later were presented to me by their writers, bound in white kid (the letters, not the authors, of course).

From Thomas Harbison,
Late Engineer of Bridges,
Peruvian Trunk Lines,
South America

To Henry Llewellyn,
Care of Union Nitrate Company,
Iquique, Chili.

Dear Old Man:

I think I was fully a week trying to drive out of my mind my last glimpse of you with your sickly grin, pretending to be tickled to pieces that the only white man within two hundred miles of your shack was going on a holiday. You old bluffer! I used to hang over the rail of the steamer, on the way up, and see you standing as I left you beside the car with its mule and the Indian driver, and behind you a million miles of soul-destroying pampa. Never mind, Jack; I sent yesterday by mail steamer the cigarettes, pipes and tobacco, canned goods and poker chips. Put in some magazines, too, and the collars. Don't know about the ties — guess it won't matter down there.

Nothing happened on the trip. One of the engines broke down three days out, and I spent all my time below decks for forty-eight hours. Chief engineer raving with D.T.'s. Got the engine fixed in record time, and haven't got my hands clean yet. It was bully.

With this I send the papers, which will tell you how I happen to be here, and why I have leisure to write you three days after landing. If the situation were not so ridiculous, it would be maddening. Here I am, off for a holiday and congratulating myself that I am foot free and heart free — yes, my friend, heart free — here I am, shut in the house of a man I never saw until last night, and wouldn't care if I never saw again, with a lot of people who never heard of me, who are almost equally vague about South America, who play as hard at bridge as I ever worked at building one (forgive this, won't you? The novelty has gone to my head), and who belong to the very class of extravagant, luxury-loving, non-producing parasites (isn't that what we called them?) that you and I used to revile from our lofty Andean pinnacle.

To come down to earth: here we are, six women and five men, including a policeman, not a servant in the house, and no one who knows how to do anything. They are really immensely interesting, these people; they all know each other very well, and it is "Jimmy" here, and "Dal" there — Dallas Brown, who went to India with me, you remember my speaking of him — and they are good natured, too, except at meal times. The little hostess, Mrs. Wilson, took over the cooking, and although luncheon was better than breakfast, the food still leaves much to the imagination.

I wish you could see this Mrs. Wilson, Hal. You would change a whole lot of your ideas. She is a thoroughbred, sure enough, and of course some of her beauty is the result of the exquisite care about which you and I — still from our Andean pinnacle — used to rant. But the fact is, she is more than that. She has fire, and pluck, no end. If you could have seen her this morning, standing in front of a cold kitchen range, determined to conquer it, and had seen the tilt of her chin when I offered to take over the cooking — you needn't grin; I can cook, and you know it — you would understand what

I mean. It was so clear that she was paralyzed with fright at the idea of getting breakfast, and equally clear that she meant to do it. By the way, I have learned that her name was McNair before she married this would-be artist, Wilson, and that she is a daughter of the McNair who financed the Callao branch!

I have not met the others so intimately. There are two sisters named Mercer, inclined to be noisy — they are playing roulette in the next room now. One is small and dark, almost Hebraic in type, named Leila and called Lollie. The other, larger, very blonde and languishing, and with a decided preference for masculine society, even, saving the mark, mine! Dallas Brown's wife, good looking, smokes cigarettes when I am not around — they all do, except Mrs. Wilson.

Then there is a maiden aunt, who is ill today with grippe and excitement, and a Miss Knowles, who came for a moment last night to see Mrs. Wilson, was caught in the quarantine (see papers), and, after hiding all night in the basement, is sulking all day in her room. Her presence created an excitement out of all proportion to the apparent cause.

From the fact that I have reason to know that my artist host and his beautiful wife are on bad terms, and from the significant glances with which the announcement of Miss Knowles' presence was met, the state of affairs seems rather clear. Wilson impresses me as a spineless sort, anyhow, and when the lady of the basement shut herself away from the rest today and I happened on "Jimmy," as they call him, pleading with her through the door, I very nearly kicked him down the stairs. Oh, yes, I'll keep out, right enough; it isn't my affair.

By the way, after the quarantine and with the policeman locked in the furnace room, a pearl necklace and a diamond bracelet were stolen! Just ten of us to divide the suspicion! Upon my word, Hal, it's the queerest situation I ever heard of. Which of us did it? I make a guess that not a few of us are fools, but which is the knave? The worst of it is, I am the only unaccredited member of the household!

This is more scandal than I ever wrote in my life. Lay it to circumscribed environment, and the lack of twenty miles over the pampa before breakfast. We have all been vaccinated, and the officious gentlemen from the board of health have taken their grins and their formaldehyde and gone. Ye gods, how we cough!

The Carlton order will go through all right, I think. Phoned him this morning. If it does, old man, we will take a month in September and explore the Mercator property.

Do you know, Hal, I have been thinking lately that you and I stick too close to the grind. Business is right enough, but what's the use of spending one's best years succeeding in everything except the things that are worth while? I'll be thirty sooner than I care to say, and — oh, well, you won't understand. You'll sit down there, with the Southern Cross and the rest of the infernal astronomical galaxy looking down on you, and the Indians chanting in the village, and you will think I have grown sentimental. I have not. You and I down there have been looking at the world through the reverse end of the glass. It's a bully old world, Hal, and this is God's part of it.

Burn this letter after you read it; I suspect it is covered with germs. Well, happy days, old man.

Yours, Tom

P.S. By the way, can't you spare some of the Indian pottery you picked up at Callao? I told Mrs. Wilson about it, and she was immensely interested. Send it to this address. Can you get it to the next steamer? — T.

FROM MAXWELL REED

To RICHARD BURTON BAGLEY,
UNIVERSITY CLUB, NEW YORK.

Dear Dick:

Enclosed find my check for five hundred, as per wager. Possibly you were within your rights in protecting your bet in the manner you chose, but while I do not wish to be offensive, your reporters are damnably so.

Yours, Maxwell Reed

FROM OFFICER FLANNIGAN

To MRS. MAGGIE FLANNIGAN, ERIN STREET.

Dear Maggie:

As soon as you receive this, go down to Mac and tell him the story as I tell you hear. Tell him I was walkin' my beat, and I'd been afther seein' Jimmy Alverini about doin' the right thing for Mac on Monday, at the poles, when I seen a man hangin' suspicious around this house, which is Mr. Wilson's, on Ninety-fifth. And, of coorse, afther chasin' the man a mile or more, I lose him, which was not my fault. So I go back to the Wilson house, and tell them to be careful about closin' up fer the night, and while I'm standin' in the hall, with all the swells around me, sparklin' with jewels, the board of health sends a man to lock us all in, because the Jap thats been waiter has took the smallpox and gone to the hospitle. I stood me ground. I sez, sez I, you cant shtop an officer in pursute of his duty. I rafuse to be shut in. Be shure to tell Mac that.

So here I am, and like to be for a month. Tell Mac theres four votes shut up here, and I can get them for him, if he can stop this monkey business.

Then go over to the Dago Church on Webster Avenue and put a dollar in Saint Anthony's box. He'll see me out of this scrape, right enough. Do it at once. Now remember, go to Mac first; maybe you can get the dollar from him, and mind what you tell him.

Your husband, Tim Flannigan

FROM ME

To MOTHER — MRS. THEODORE MCNAIR,
HOTEL HAMILTON, BERMUDA.
Dearest Mother:

I hope you will get this before you read the papers, and when you *do* read them, you are not to get excited and worried. I am as well as can be, and a great deal safer than I ever remember to have been in my life. We are quarantined, a lot of us, in Jim Wilson's house, because his irreproachable Jap did a very reproachable thing — took smallpox. Now read on before you get excited. *His room has been fumigated,* and we have been vaccinated. I am well and happy. I can't be killed in a railway wreck or smashed when the car skids. Unless I drown myself in my bath, or jump through a window, positively nothing can happen to me. So gather up all your maternal anxieties and cast them to the Bermuda sharks.

Anne Brown is here — see the papers for list — and if she can not play propriety, Jimmy's Aunt Selina can. In fact, she doesn't play at it; she works. I have telephoned Lizette for some clothes — enough for a couple of weeks, although Dallas promises to get us out sooner. Now, dear, do go ahead and have a nice time, and on no account come home. You could only have the carriage to stop in front of the house, and wave to me through a window.

Mother, I want you to do something for me. You know who is down there, and — this is awfully delicate, Mumsy — but he's a nice boy, and I thought I liked him. I guess you know he has been rather attentive. Now, I *do* like him, Mumsy, but not the way I thought I did, and I want you to — very gently, of course — to discourage him a little. You know how I mean. He's a dear boy, but I am so tired of people who don't know anything but horses and motors.

And, oh, yes, — do you remember a girl named Lucille Mellon who was at school with you in Rome? And that she married a man named Harbison? Well, her son is here! He builds railroads and bridges and things, and he even built himself an automobile down in South America, because he couldn't afford to buy one, and burned wood in it! Wood! Think of it!

I wired father in Chicago for fear he would come rushing home. The picture in the paper of the face at the basement window is supposed to be Mr. Harbison, but of course it isn't anymore like him than mine is like me.

Anne Brown mislaid her pearl collar when she took it off last night, and has fussed herself into a sick headache. She declares it was stolen! Some of the people are playing bridge, Betty Mercer is doing a cake walk to the *Rhapsodie Hongroise* — Jim has no everyday music — and the telephone is ringing. We have received enough flowers for a funeral — somebody sent Lollie a Gates Ajar, only with the gates shut.

There are no servants — think of it, Mumsy. I wish you had made me learn to cook. Mr. Harbison has shown me a little — he was a soldier in the Spanish War — but we girls are a terribly ignorant lot, Mumsy, about the real things of life.

Now, don't worry. It is more sport than camping in the

Adirondacks, and not nearly so damp.

Your loving daughter, Katherine.

P.S. — South America must be wonderful. Why can't we put the Gadfly in commission, and take a coasting trip this summer? It is a shame to own a yacht and never use it. K.

THIS NOTE, EVIDENTLY DELIVERED BY MESSENGER, WAS FOUND AMONG OTHER LITTER IN THE VESTIBULE, AFTER THE LIFTING OF THE QUARANTINE.

Mr. Alex Dodds, City Editor, Mail and Star:

Dear D. —

Can't get a picture. Have waited seven hours. They have closed the shutters.

McCord.

WRITTEN ON THE BACK OF THE ABOVE NOTE.

Watch the roof.

Dodds.

Chapter IX

FLANNIGAN'S FIND

*T*he most charitable thing would be to say nothing about the first day. We were baldly brutal — that's the only word for it. And Mr. Harbison, with his beautiful courtesy — the really sincere kind — tried to patch up one quarrel after another and failed. He rose superbly to the occasion, and made something that he called a South American goulash for luncheon, although it was too salty, and everyone was thirsty the rest of the day.

Bella was horrid, of course. She froze Jim until he said he was going to sit in the refrigerator and cool the butter. She locked herself in the dressing room — it had been assigned to me, but that made no difference to Bella — and did her nails, and took three different baths, and refused to come to the table. And of course Jimmy was wild, and said she would starve. But I said, "Very well, let her starve. Not a tray shall leave my kitchen." It was a comfort to have her shut up there anyhow; it postponed the time when she would come face to face with Flannigan.

Aunt Selina got sick that day, as I have said. I was not so bitter as the others; I did not say that I wished she would die. The worst I ever wished her was that she might be quite ill for some time, and yet, when she began to recover, she was dreadful to me. She said for one thing, that it was the hard-boiled eggs and the state of the house that did it, and when I said that the grippe was a germ, she retorted that I had probably brought it to her on my clothing.

You remember that Betty had drawn the nurse's slip, and how pleased she had been about it. She got up early the morning of the first day and made herself a lawn cap and telephoned out for a white nurse's uniform — that is, of course, for a white uniform for a nurse. She really looked very fetching, and she went around all the morning with a red cross on her sleeve and a Saint Cecilia expression, gathering up bottles of medicine — most of it flesh reducer, which was pathetic, and closing windows for fear of drafts. She refused to help with the house work, and looked quite exalted, but by afternoon it had palled on her somewhat, and she and Max shook dice.

Betty was really pleased when Aunt Selina sent for her. She took in a bottle of cologne to bathe her brow, and we all stood outside the door and listened. Betty tiptoed in in her pretty cap and apron, and we heard her cautiously draw down the shades.

"What are you doing that for?" Aunt Selina demanded. "I like the light."

"It's bad for your poor eyes," Betty's tone was exactly the proper bedside pitch, low and sugary.

"Sweet and low, sweet and low, wind of the western sea!" Dal hummed outside.

"Put up those window shades!" Aunt Selina's voice was strong enough. "What's in that bottle?"

Betty was still mild. She swished to the window and raised the shade.

"I'm *so* sorry you are ill," she said sympathetically. "This is for your poor aching head. Now close your eyes and lie perfectly still, and I will cool your forehead."

"There's nothing the matter with my head," Aunt Selina retorted. "And I have not lost my faculties; I am not a child or a sick cow. If that's perfumery, take it out."

We heard Betty coming to the door, but there was no time to get away. She had dropped her mask for a minute and was biting her lip, but when she saw us she forced a smile.

"She's ill, poor dear," she said. "If you people will go away, I can bring her around all right. In two hours she will eat out of my hand."

"Eat a piece out of your hand," Max scoffed in a whisper.

We waited a little longer, but it was too painful. Aunt Selina demanded a mustard foot bath and a hot lemonade and her back rubbed with liniment and some strong black tea. And in the intervals she wanted to be read to out of the prayer book. And when we had all gone away, there came the most terrible noise from Aunt Selina's room, and everyone ran. We found Betty in the hall outside the door, crying, with her fingers in her ears and her cap over her eye. She said she had been putting the hot water bottle to Aunt Selina's back, and it had been too hot. Just then something hit against the door with a soft thud, fell to the floor and burst, for a trickle of hot water came over the sill.

"She won't let me hold her hand," Betty wailed, "or bathe her brow, or smooth her pillow. She thinks of nothing but her stomach or her back! And when I try to make her bed look decent, she spits at me like a cat. Everything I do is wrong. She spilled the foot bath into her shoes, and blamed me for it."

It took the united efforts of all of us — except Bella, who stood back and smiled nastily — to get Betty back into the sick room again. I was supremely thankful by that time that I had not drawn the nurse's slip. With dinner ordered in from one of the clubs, and the omelet ten hours behind me, my position did not seem so unbearable. But a new development was coming.

While Betty was fussing with Aunt Selina, Max led a search of the house. He said the necklace and the bracelet must be hidden somewhere, and that no crevice was too small to neglect.

We made a formal search all together, except Betty and Aunt Selina, and we found a lot of things in different places that Jim said had been missing since the year one. But no jewels — nothing even suggesting a jewel was found. We had explored the entire house, every cupboard, every chest, even the insides of the couches and the pockets of Jim's clothes — which he resented bitterly — and found nothing, and I must say the situation was growing rather strained. Some one had taken the jewels; they hadn't walked away.

It was Flannigan who suggested the roof, and as we had tried every place else, we climbed there. Of course we didn't find anything, but after all day in the house with the shutters closed on account of reporters, the air was glorious. It was February, but quite mild and sunny, and we could look down over Riverside Drive and the Hudson, and even recognize people we knew on horseback and in cars. It was a pathetic joy, and we lined up along the parapet and watched the motor boats racing on the river, and tried to feel that we were in the world as well as of it, but it was very hard.

Betty had been making tea for Aunt Selina, and of course when she heard us up there, she followed, tray and all, and we drank Aunt Selina's tea and had the first really nice time of the day. Bella had come up, too, but she was still standoffish and queer, and she stood leaning against a chimney and staring out over the river. After a little Mr. Harbison put down his cup and went over to her, and they talked quite confidentially for a long time. I thought it bad taste in Bella, under the circumstances, after snubbing Dallas and Max, and of course treating Jim like the dirt under her feet, to turn right around and be lovely to Mr. Harbison. It was hard for Jim.

Max came and sat beside me, and Flannigan, who had been sent down for more cups, passed tea, putting the tray on top of the chimney. Jim was sitting grumpily on the roof, with his feet folded under him, playing Canfield in the shadow of the parapet, buying the deck out of one pocket and putting his winnings in the other. He was watching Bella, too, and she knew it, and she strained a point to captivate Mr. Harbison. Anyone could see that.

And that was the picture that came out in the next morning's papers, tea cups, cards and all. For when some one looked up, there were four newspaper photographers on the roof of the next house, and they had the impertinence to thank us!

Flannigan had seen Bella by that time, but as he still didn't understand the situation, things were just the same. But his manner to me puzzled me; whenever he came near me he winked prodigiously, and during all the search he kept one eye on me, and seemed to be amused about something.

When the rest had gone down to dress for dinner, which was being sent in, thank goodness, I still sat on the parapet and watched the darkening river. I felt terribly lonely, all at once, and sad. There wasn't anyone any nearer than father, in the West, or mother in Bermuda, who really cared a rap whether I sat on that parapet all night or not, or who would be sorry if I leaped to the dirty bricks of the next door-yard — not that I meant to, of course.

The lights came out across the river, and made purple and yellow streaks on the water, and one of the motor boats came panting back to the yacht club, coughing and gasping as if it had overdone. Down on the street automobiles were starting and stopping, cabs rolling, doors slamming, all the maddening, delightful bustle of people who are foot-free to dine out, to dance, to go to the theater, to do any of the thousand possibilities of a long February evening. And above them I sat on the roof and cried. Yes, cried.

I was roused by some one coughing just behind me, and I tried to straighten my face before I turned. It was Flannigan, his double row of brass buttons gleaming in the twilight.

"Excuse me, miss," he said affably, "but the boy from the hotel has left the dinner on the doorstep and run, the cowardly little divil! What'll I do with it? I went to Mrs. Wilson, but she says it's no concern of hers." Flannigan was evidently bewildered.

"You'd better keep it warm, Flannigan," I replied. "You needn't wait; I'm coming." But he did not go.

"If — if you'll excuse me, miss," he said, "don't you think ye'd betther tell them?"

"Tell them what?"

"The whole thing — the joke," he said confidentially, coming closer. "It's been great sport, now, hasn't it? But I'm afraid they will get on to it soon, and — some of them might not be agreeable. A pearl necklace is a pearl necklace, miss, and the lady's wild."

"What do you mean?" I gasped. "You don't think — why, Flannigan —"

He merely grinned at me and thrust his hand down in his pocket. When he brought it up he had Bella's bracelet on his palm, glittering in the faint light.

"Where did you get it?" Between relief and the absurdity of the thing, I was almost hysterical. But Flannigan did not give me the bracelet; instead, it struck me his tone was suddenly severe.

"Now look here, miss," he said; "you've played your trick, and you've had your fun. The Lord knows it's only folks like you would play April fool jokes with a fortune! If you're the sinsible little woman you look to be, you'll put that pearl collar on the coal in the basement tonight, and let me find it."

"I haven't got the pearl collar," I protested. "I think you are crazy. Where did you get that bracelet?"

He edged away from me, as if he expected me to snatch it from him and run, but he was still trying in an elephantine way to treat the matter as a joke.

"I found it in a drawer in the pantry," he said, "among the dirty linen. And if you're as smart as I think you are, I'll find the pearl collar there in the morning — and nothing said, miss."

So there I was, suspected of being responsible for Anne's pearl collar, as if I had not enough to worry me before. Of course I could have called them all together and told them, and made them explain to Flannigan what I had really meant by my delirious speech in the kitchen. But that would have meant telling the whole ridiculous story to Mr. Harbison, and having him think us all mad, and me a fool.

In all that overcrowded house there was only one place where I could be miserable with comfort. So I stayed on the roof, and cried a little and then became angry and walked up and down, and clenched my hands and babbled helplessly. The boats on the river were yellow, horizontal streaks through my tears, and an early searchlight sent its shaft like a tangible thing in the darkness, just over my head. Then, finally, I curled down in a corner with my arms on the parapet, and the lights became more and more prismatic and finally formed themselves into a circle that was Bella's bracelet, and that kept whirling around and around on something flat and not overclean, that was Flannigan's palm.

Chapter X

ON THE STAIRS

I was roused by someone walking across the roof, the cracking of tin under feet, and a comfortable and companionable odor of tobacco. I moved a very little, and then I saw that it was a man — the height and erectness told me which man. And just at that instant he saw me.

"Good Lord!" he ejaculated, and throwing his cigar away he came across quickly. "Why, Mrs. Wilson, what in the world are you doing here? I thought — they said —"

"That I was sulking again?" I finished disagreeably. "Perhaps I am. In fact, I'm quite sure of it."

"You are not," he said severely. "You have been asleep in a February night, in the open air, with less clothing on than I wear in the tropics."

I had got up by this time, refusing his help, and because my feet were numb, I sat down on the parapet for a moment. Oh, I knew what I looked like — one of those "Valley-of-the-Nile-After-a-Flood" pictures.

"There is one thing about you that is comforting," I sniffed. "You said precisely the same thing to me at three o'clock this morning. You never startle me by saying anything unexpected."

He took a step toward me, and even in the dusk I could see that he was looking down at me oddly. All my bravado faded away and there was a queerish ringing in my ears.

"I would like to!" he said tensely. "I would like, this minute — I'm a fool, Mrs. Wilson," he finished miserably. "I ought to be drawn and quartered, but when I see you like this I — I get crazy. If you say the word, I'll — I'll go down and —" He clenched his fist.

It was reprehensible, of course; he saw that in an instant, for he shut his teeth over something that sounded very fierce, and strode away from me, to stand looking out over the river, with his hands thrust in his pockets. Of course the thing I should have done was to ignore what he had said altogether, but he was so uncomfortable, so chastened, that, feline, feminine, whatever the instinct is, I could not let him go. I had been so wretched myself.

"What is it you would like to say?" I called over to him. He did not speak. "Would you tell me that I am a silly child for pouting?" No reply; he struck a match. "Or would you preach a nice little sermon about people — about women — loving their husbands?"

He grunted savagely under his breath.

"Be quite honest," I pursued relentlessly. "Say that we are a lot of barbarians, say that because my — because Jimmy treats me outrageously — oh, he does; anyone can see that — and because I loathe him — and anyone can tell that — why don't you say you are shocked to the depths?" I was a little shocked myself by that time, but I couldn't stop, having started.

He came over to me, white-faced and towering, and he had the audacity to grip my arm and stand me on my feet, like a bad child — which I was, I dare say.

"Don't!" he said in a husky, very pained voice. "You are only talking; you don't mean it. It isn't *you*. You know you care, or else why are you crying up here? And don't do it again, *don't do it again* — or I will —"

"You will — what?"

"Make a fool of myself, as I have now," he finished grimly. And then he stalked away and left me there alone, completely bewildered, to find my way down in the dark.

I groped along, holding to the rail, for the staircase to the roof was very steep, and I went slowly. Half-way down the stairs there was a tiny landing, and I stopped. I could have sworn I heard Mr. Harbison's footsteps far below, growing fainter. I even smiled a little, there in the dark, although I had been rather profoundly shaken. The next instant I knew I had been wrong; some one was on the landing with me. I could hear short, sharp breathing, and then —

I am not sure that I struggled; in fact, I don't believe I did — I was too limp with amazement. The creature, to have lain in wait for me like that! And he was brutally strong; he caught me to him fiercely, and held me there, close, and he kissed me — not once or twice, but half a dozen times, long kisses that filled me with hot shame for him, for myself, that I had — liked him. The roughness of his coat bruised my cheek; I loathed him. And then someone came whistling along the hall below, and he pushed me from him and stood listening, breathing in long, gasping breaths.

I ran; when my shaky knees would hold me, I ran. I wanted to hide my hot face, my disgust, my disillusion; I wanted to put my head in mother's lap and cry; I wanted to die, or be ill, so I need never see him again. Perversely enough, I did none of those things. With my face still flaming, with burning eyes and hands that shook, I made a belated evening toilet and went slowly, haughtily, down the stairs. My hands were like ice, but I was consumed with rage. Oh, I would show him — that this was New York, not Iquique; that the roof was not his Andean tableland.

Everyone elaborately ignored my absence from dinner. The Dallas Browns, Max and Lollie were at bridge; Jim was alone in the den, walking the floor and biting at an unlighted cigar; Betty had returned to Aunt Selina and was hysterical, they said, and Flannigan was in deep dejection because I had missed my dinner.

"Betty is making no end of a row," Max said, looking up from his game, "because the old lady upstairs insists on chloroform liniment. Betty says the smell makes her ill."

"And she can inhale Russian cigarettes," Anne said enviously, "and gasoline fumes, without turning a hair. I call a revoke, Dal; you trumped spades on the second round."

Dal flung over three tricks with very bad grace, and Anne counted them with maddening deliberation.

"Game and rubber," she said. "Watch Dal, Max; he will cheat in the score if he can. Kit, don't have another clam while I am in this house. I have eaten so many lately my waist rises and falls with the tide."

"You have a stunning color, Kit," Lollie said. "You are really quite superb. Who made that gown?"

"Where have you been hiding, du kleine?" Max whispered, under cover of showing me the evening paper, with a photograph of the house and a cross at the cellar window where we had tried to escape. "If one day in the house with you, Kit, puts me in this condition, what will a month do?"

From beyond the curtain of a sort of alcove, lighted with a red-shaded lamp, came a hum of conversation, Bella's cool, even tones, and a heavy masculine voice. They were laughing; I could feel my chin go up. He was not even hiding his shame.

"Max," I asked, while the others clamored for him and the game, "has anyone been up through the house since dinner? Any of the men?"

He looked at me curiously.

"Only Harbison," he replied promptly. "Jim has been eating his heart out in the den every since dinner; Dal played the Sonata Appasionata backward on the pianola — he wanted to put through one of Anne's lingerie waists, on a wager that it would play a tune; I played craps with Lollie, and Flannigan has been washing dishes. Why?"

Well, that was conclusive, anyhow. I had had a faint hope that it might have been a joke, although it had borne all the evidences of sincerity, certainly. But it was past doubting now; he had lain in wait for me at the landing, and had kissed me, *me*, when he thought I was Jimmy's wife. Oh, I must have been very light, very contemptible, if that was what he thought of me!

I went into the library and got a book, but it was impossible to read, with Jimmy lying on the couch giving vent to something between a sigh and a groan every few minutes. About eleven the cards stopped, and Bella said she would read palms. She began with Mr. Harbison, because she declared he had a wonderful hand, full of possibilities; she said he should have been a great inventor or a playwright, and that his attitude to women was one of homage, respect, almost reverence. He had the courage to look at me, and if a glance could have killed he would have withered away.

When Jimmy proffered his hand, she looked at it icily. Of

course she could not refuse, with Mr. Harbison looking on.

"Rather negative," she said coldly. "The lines are obscured by cushions of flesh; no heart line at all, mentality small, self-indulgence and irritability very marked."

Jim held his palm up to the light and stared at it.

"Gad!" he said. "Hardly safe for me to go around without gloves, is it?"

It was all well enough for Jim to laugh, but he was horribly hurt. He stood around for a few minutes, talking to Anne, but as soon as he could he slid away and went to bed. He looked very badly the next morning, as though he had not slept, and his clothes quite hung on him. He was actually thinner. But that is ahead of the story.

Max came to me while the others were sitting around drinking nightcaps, and asked me in a low tone if he could see me in the den; he wanted to ask me something. Dal overheard.

"Ask her here," he said. "We all know what it is, Max. Go ahead and we'll coach you."

"Will you coach *me*?" I asked, for Mr. Harbison was listening.

"The woman does not need it," Dal retorted. And then, because Max looked angry enough really to propose to me right there, I got up hastily and went into the den. Max followed, and closing the door, stood with his back against it.

"Contrary to the general belief, Kit," he began, "I did *not* intend to ask you to marry me."

I breathed easier. He took a couple of steps toward me and stood with his arms folded, looking down at me. "I'm not at all sure, in fact, that I shall ever propose to you," he went on unpleasantly.

"You have already done it twice. You are not going to take those back, are you, Max?" I asked, looking up at him.

But Max was not to be cajoled. He came close and stood with his hand on the back of my chair. "What happened on the roof tonight?" He demanded hoarsely.

"I do not think it would interest you," I retorted, coloring in spite of myself.

"Not interest me! I am shut in this blasted house; I have

to see the only woman I ever loved — *really* loved," he supplemented, as he caught my eye, "pretend she is another man's wife. Then I sit back and watch her using every art — all her beauty — to make still another man love her, a man who thinks she is a married woman. If Harbison were worth the trouble, I would tell him the whole story, Aunt Selina be — obliterated!"

I sat up suddenly.

"If Harbison were worth the trouble!" I repeated. What did he mean? Had he seen —

"I mean just this," Max said slowly. "There is only one unaccredited member of this household; only one person, save Flannigan, who was locked in the furnace room, one person who was awake and around the house when Anne's jewels went, only one person in the house, also, who would have any motive for the theft."

"Motive?" I asked dully.

"Poverty," Max threw at me. "Oh, I mean comparative poverty, of course. Who is this fellow, anyhow? Dal knew him at school, traveled with him through India. On the strength of that he brings him here, quarters him with decent people, and wonders when they are systematically robbed!"

"You are unjust!" I said, rising and facing him. "I do not like Mr. Harbison — I — I hate him, if you want to know. But as to his being a thief, I — think it is quite as likely that you took the necklace."

Max threw his cigarette into the fire angrily.

"So that is how it is!" he mocked. "If either of us is the thief, it is I! You *do* hate him, don't you?"

I left him there, flushed with irritation, and joined the others. Just as I entered the room, Betty burst through the hall door like a cyclone, and collapsed into a chair. "She's a mean, cantankerous old woman!" she declared, feeling for her handkerchief. "You can take care of your own Aunt Selina, Jim Wilson. I will never go near her again."

"What did you do? Poison her?" Dallas asked with interest.

"G—— got camphor in her eyes," snuffed Betty. "You never — heard such a noise. I wouldn't be a trained nurse for anything in the world. She — she called me a hussy!"

"You're not going to give her up, are you, Betty?" Jim asked imploringly. But Betty was, and said so plainly.

"Anyhow, she won't have me back," she finished, "and she has sent for — guess!"

"Have mercy!" Dal cried, dropping to his knees. "Oh, fair ministering angel, she has not sent for me!"

"No," Betty said maliciously. "She wants Bella — she's crazy about her."

Chapter XI
I MAKE A DISCOVERY

*R*eally, I have left Aunt Selina rather out of it, but she was important as a cause, not as a result; at least at first. She came out strong later. I believe she was a very nice old woman, with strong likes and prejudices, which she was perfectly willing to pay for. At least, I only presume she had likes; I know she had prejudices.

Nobody every understood why Bella consented to take Betty's place with Aunt Selina. As for me, I was too much engrossed with my own affairs to pay the invalid much attention. Once or twice during the day I had stopped in to see her, and had been received frigidly and with marked disapproval. I was in disgrace, of course, after the scene in the dining room the night before. I had stood like a naughty child, just inside the door, and replied meekly when she said the pillows were overstuffed, and why didn't I have the linen slips rinsed in starch water? She laid the blame of her illness on me, as I have said before, and she made Jim read to her in the afternoon from a book she carried with her, Coals of Fire on the *domestic* Hearth, marking places for me to read.

She sent for me that night, just as I had taken off my gown; so I threw on a dressing gown and went in. To my horror, Jim was already there. At a gesture from Aunt Selina, he closed the door into the hall and tiptoed back beside the bed, where he sat staring at the figures on the silk comfort.

Aunt Selina's first words were:

"Where's that flibberty-gibbet?"

Jim looked at me.

"She must mean Betty," I explained. "She has gone to bed, I think."

"Don't — let — her — in — this — room — again," she said, with awful emphasis. "She is an infamous creature."

"Oh, come now, Aunt Selina," Jim broke in; "she's foolish, perhaps, but she's a nice little thing."

Aunt Selina's face was a curious study. Then she raised herself on her elbow, and, taking a flat chamois-skin bag from under her pillow, held it out.

"My cameo breastpin," she said solemnly; "my cuff-buttons with gold rims and storks painted on china in the middle; my watch, that has put me to bed and got me up for forty years, and my money — five hundred and ten dollars and forty cents! — taken with the doors locked under my nose." Which was ambiguous, but forcible.

"But, good gracious, Miss Car — Aunt Selina!" I exclaimed, "you don't think Betty Mercer took those things?"

"No," she said grimly; "I think I probably got up in my sleep and lighted the fire with them, or sent 'em out for a walk." Then she stuffed the bag away and sat up resolutely in bed.

"Have you made up?" she demanded, looking from one to the other of us. "Bella, don't tell me you still persist in that nonsense."

"What nonsense?" I asked, getting ready to run.

"That you do not love him."

"Him?"

"James," she snapped irritably. "Do you suppose I mean the policeman?"

I looked over at Jimmy. She had got me by the hand, and Jimmy was making frantic gestures to tell her the whole thing and be done with it. But I had gone too far. The mill of the gods had crushed me already, and I didn't propose to be drawn out hideously mangled and held up as an example for the next two or three weeks, although it was clear enough that Aunt Selina disapproved of me thoroughly, and would have been glad enough to find that no tie save the board of health held us together. And then Bella came in, and you wouldn't have known her. She had put on a straight white woolen wrapper, and she had her hair in two long braids down her back. She looked like a nice, wide-eyed little girl in her teens, and she had some lobster salad and a glass of port on a tray. When she saw the situation, she put the things down and had the nastiness to stay and listen.

"I'm not blind," Aunt Selina said, with one eye on the tray. "You two silly children adore each other; I saw some things last night."

Bella took a step forward; then she stopped and shrugged her shoulders. Jim was purple.

"I saw you kiss her in the dining room, remember that!" Aunt Selina went on, giving the screw another turn.

It was Bella's turn to be excited. She gave me one awful stare, then she fixed her eyes on Jim.

"Besides," Aunt Selina went on, "you told me today that you loved her. Don't deny it, James."

Bella couldn't keep quiet another instant. She came over and stood at the foot of the bed.

"Please don't excite yourself, *dear* Miss Caruthers," she said in a voice like ice. "Everyone knows that he loves her; he simply overflows with it. It — it is quite a by-word among their friends. They have been sitting together in a corner all evening."

Yes, that was what she said; when I had not spoken to Jimmy the whole time in the den. Bella was cattish, and she was jealous, too. I turned on my heel and went to the door; then I turned to her, with my hand on the knob.

"You have been misinformed," I said coldly. "You can not possibly know, having spent three hours in a corner yourself — with Mr. Harbison." I abhor jealousy in a woman.

Well, Aunt Selina ate all the lobster salad, and drank the port after Bella had told her it was beef, iron and wine, and she slept all night, and was able to sit up in a chair the next day, and was so infatuated with Bella that she would not let her out of her sight. But that is ahead of the story.

At midnight the house was fairly quiet, except for Jim, who kept walking around the halls because he couldn't sleep. I got up at last and ordered him to bed, and he had the audacity to have a grievance with me.

"Look at my situation now!" he said, sitting pensively on

a steam radiator. "Aunt Selina is crazy. I only kissed your hand, anyhow, and I don't know why you sat in the den all evening; you might have known that Bella would notice it. Why couldn't you leave me alone to my misery?"

"Very well," I said, much offended. "After this I shall sit with Flannigan in the kitchen. He is the only gentleman in the house."

I left him babbling apologies and went to bed, but I had an uncomfortable feeling that Bella had been a witness to our conversation, for the door into Aunt Selina's room closed softly as I passed.

I knew beforehand that I was not going to sleep. The instant I turned out the light the nightmare events of the evening ranged themselves in a procession, or a series of tableaus, one after the other; Flannigan on the roof, with the bracelet on his palm, looking accusingly at me; Mr. Harbison and the scene on the roof, with my flippancy; and the result of that flippancy — the man on the stairs, the arms that held me, the terrible kisses that had scorched my lips — it was awful! And then the absurd situation across Aunt Selina's bed, and Bella's face! Oh, it was all so ridiculous — my having thought that the Harbison man was a gentleman, and finding him a cad, and worse. It was excruciatingly funny. I quite got a headache from laughing; indeed I laughed until I found I was crying, and then I knew I was going to have an attack of strangulated emotion, called hysteria. So I got up and turned on all the lights, and bathed my face with cologne, and felt better.

But I did not go to sleep. When the hall clock chimed two, I discovered I was hungry. I had had nothing since luncheon, and even the thirst following the South American goulash was gone. There was probably something to eat in the pantry, and if there was not, I was quite equal to going to the basement.

As it happened, however, I found a very orderly assortment of left-overs and a pitcher of milk, which had no business there in the pantry, and with plenty of light I was not at all frightened.

I ate bread and butter and drank milk, and was fast becoming a rational person again; I had pulled out one of the drawers part way, and with a tray across the corner I had improvised a comfortable seat. And then I noticed that the drawer was full of soiled napkins, and I remembered the bracelet. I hardly know why I decided to go through the drawer again, after Flannigan had already done it, but I did. I finished my milk and then, getting down on my knees, I proceeded systematically to empty the drawer. I took out perhaps a dozen napkins and as many doilies without finding anything. Then I took out a large tray cloth, and there was something on it that made me look farther. One corner of it had been scorched, the clear and well defined imprint of a lighted cigarette or cigar, a blackened streak that trailed off into a brown and yellow. I had a queer, trembly feeling, as if I were on the brink of a discovery — perhaps Anne's pearls, or the cuff buttons with storks painted on china in the center. But the only thing I found, down in the corner of the drawer, was a half-burned cigarette.

To me, it seemed quite enough. It was one of the South American cigarettes, with a tobacco wrapper instead of paper, that Mr. Harbison smoked.

Chapter XII
THE ROOF GARDEN

I was quite ill the next morning — from excitement, I suppose. Anyhow, I did not get up, and there wasn't any breakfast. Jim said he roused Flannigan at eight o'clock, to go down and get the fire started, and then went back to bed. But Flannigan did not get up. He appeared, sheepishly, at half-past ten, and by that time Bella was down, in a towering rage, and had burned her hand and got the fire started, and had taken up a tray for Aunt Selina and herself.

As the others straggled down they boiled themselves eggs or ate fruit, and nobody put anything away. Lollie Mercer made me some tea and scorched toast, and brought it, about eleven o'clock.

"I never saw such a house," she declared. "A dozen house-maids couldn't put it in order. Why should every man that smokes drop ashes wherever he happens to be?"

"That's the question of the ages," I replied languidly. "What was Max talking so horribly about a little while ago?" Lollie looked up aggrieved.

"About nothing at all," she declared. "Anne told me to clean the bath tubs with oil, and I did it, that's all. Now Max says he couldn't get it off, and his clothes stick to him, and if he should forget and strike a match in the — in the usual way, he would explode. He can clean his own tub tomorrow," she finished vindictively.

At noon Jim came in to see me, bringing Anne as a concession to Bella. He was in a rage, and he carried the morning paper like a club in his hand.

"What sort of a newspaper lie would you call this?" he demanded irritably. "It makes me crazy; everybody with a mental image of me leaning over the parapet of the roof, waving a board, with the rest of you sitting on my legs to keep me from overbalancing!"

"Maybe there's a picture!" Anne said hopefully.

Jim looked.

"No picture," he announced. "I wonder why they restrained themselves! I wish Bella would keep off the roof," he added, with fresh access of rage, "or wear a mask or veil. One of those fellows is going to recognize her, and there'll be the deuce to pay."

"When you are all through discussing this thing, perhaps you will tell me what is the matter," I remarked from my couch. "Why did you lean over the parapet, Jim, and who sat on your legs?"

"I didn't; nobody did," he retorted, waving the newspaper. "It's a lie out of the whole cloth, that's what it is. I asked you girls to be decent to those reporters; it never pays to offend a newspaper man. Listen to this, Kit."

He read the article rapidly, furiously, pausing every now and then to make an exasperated comment.

Attempt at Escape
Frustrated Members of the Four Hundred Defy the Law

"Special Officer McCloud, on duty at the quarantined house of James Wilson, artist and clubman, on Ninety-fifth Street, reported this morning a daring attempt at escape, made at 3 A.M. It is in this house that some eight or nine members of the smart set were imprisoned during the course of a dinner party, when the Japanese butler developed smallpox. The party shut in the house includes Miss Katherine McNair, the daughter of Theodore McNair, of the Inter-Ocean system; Mr. and Mrs. Dallas Brown; the Misses Mercer; Maxwell Reed, the well-known clubman and whip; and a Mr. Thomas Harbison, guest of the Dallas Browns and a South American.

"Officer McCloud's story, told to a Chronicle reporter this morning, is as follows: The occupants of the house had been uneasy all day. From the air of subdued bustle, and from a careful inspection of the roof, made by the entire party during the afternoon, his suspicion had been aroused. Nothing unusual, however, occurred during the early part of the night. From eight o'clock to twelve, McCloud was relieved from duty, his place being taken by Michael Shane, of the Eighty-sixth Street Station.

"When McCloud came on duty at midnight, Shane reported that about eleven o'clock the searchlight of a steamer on the river, flashing over the house, had shown a man crouching on the parapet, evidently surveying the roof across, which at this point is only twelve feet distant, with a view of making his escape. One seeing Shane below, however, he had beat a retreat, but not before the officer had seen him distinctly. He was dressed in evening clothes and wore a light tan overcoat.

"Officer McCloud relieved Shane at midnight, and sent for a plain-clothes man from the station house. This man was stationed on the roof of the Bevington residence next door, with strict injunctions to prevent an escape from the quarantined mansion. Nothing suspicious having occurred, the man on the roof left about 3 A.M., reporting to McCloud below that everything was quiet. At that moment, glancing skyward, one of the officers was astounded to see a long narrow board project itself from the coping of the Wildon house, waver uncertainly for a moment, and then advance stealthily toward the parapet across. When it was within a foot or two of a resting place, McCloud called sharply to the invisible refugee above, at the same time firing his revolver in the ground.

"The result was surprising. The board stopped, trembled, swayed a little, and dropped, missing the vigilant officers by a hair's breadth, and crashing to the cement with a terrific force. An inspection of the roof from the Bevington house, later, revealed nothing unusual. It is evident, however, that the quarantine is proving irksome to the inhabitants of the sequestered residence, most of whom are typical society folk, without resources in themselves. Their condition, without valets and maids, is certainly pitiable. It has been rumored that the ladies are doing their own hair, and that the gentlemen have been reduced to putting their own buttons in their shirts. This deplorable situation, however, is unavoidable.

"The vigilance of the board of health has been most commendable in this case. Beginning with a wager over the telephone that they would break quarantine in twenty-four hours, and ending with the attempt to span a twelve-foot gulf with a board, over which to cross to freedom, these shut-in society folk have shown characteristic disregard of the laws of the state. It is quite time to extend to the millionaire the same strictness that keeps the commuter at home for three weeks with the measles; that makes him get the milk bottles and groceries from the gate post and smell like dog soap for a month afterward, as a result of disinfection.'"

We sat in dead silence for a minute. Then:

"Perhaps it is true," I said. "Not of you, Jim — but some one may have tried to get out that way. In fact, I think it extremely likely."

"Who? Flannigan? You couldn't drive him out. He's having the time of his life. Do you suspect me?"

"Come away and don't fight," Anne broke in pacifically. "You will have to have luncheon sent in, Jimmy; nobody has ordered anything from the shops, and I feel like old Mother Hubbard."

"I wish you would all go out," I said wearily. "If every man in the house says he didn't try to get over to the next roof last night, well and good. But you might look and see if the board is still lying where it fell."

There was an instantaneous rush for the window, and a second's pause. Then Jimmy's voice, incredulous, awed:

"Well, I'll be — blessed! There's the board!"

I stayed in my room all that day. My head really ached and then, too, I did not care to meet Mr. Harbison. It would have to come; I realized that a meeting was inevitable, but I wanted time to think how I would meet him. It would be impossible to cut him, without rousing the curiosity of the others to fever pitch; and it was equally impossible to ignore the disgraceful episode on the stairs. As it happened, however, I need not have worried. I went down to dinner, languidly, when everyone was seated, and found Max at my right, and Mr. Harbison moved over beside Bella. Everyone was talking at once, for Flannigan, ambling around the table as airily as he walked his beat, had presented Bella with her bracelet on a salad plate, garnished with romaine. He had found it in the furnace room, he said, where she must have dropped it. And he looked at me stealthily, to approve his mendacity!

Everyone was famished, and as they ate they discussed the board in the area way, and pretended to deride it as a clever bit of press work, to revive a dying sensation. No one was deceived; Anne's pearls and the attempt to escape, coming just after, pointed only to one thing. I looked around the table, dazed. Flannigan, almost the only unknown quantity, might have tried to escape the night before, but he would not have been in dress clothes. Besides, he must be eliminated as far as the pearls were concerned, having been locked in the furnace room the night they were stolen. There was no one among the girls to suspect. The Mercer girls had stunning pearls, and could secure all they wanted legitimately; and Bella disliked them. Oh, there was no question about it, I decided; Dallas and Anne had taken a wolf to their bosom — or is it a viper? — and the Harbison man was the creature. Although I must say that, looking over the table, at Jimmy's breadth and not very imposing personality, at Max's lean length, sallow skin, and bold dark eyes, at Dallas, blond, growing bald and florid, and then at the Harbison boy, tall, muscular, clear-eyed and sunburned, one would have taken Max at first choice as the villain, with Dal next, Jim third, and the Harbison boy not in the running.

It was just after dinner that the surprise was sprung on me. Mr. Harbison came around to me gravely, and asked me if I felt able to go up on the roof. On the roof, after last night! I had to gather myself together; luckily, the others were pushing back their chairs, showing Flannigan the liqueur glasses to take up, and lighting cigars.

"I do not care to go," I said icily.

"The others are coming," he persisted, "and I — I could give you an arm up the stairs."

"I believe you are good at that," I said, looking at him steadily. "Max, will you help me to the roof?"

Mr. Harbison really turned rather white. Then he bowed ceremoniously and left me.

Max got me a wrap, and everyone except Mr. Harbison and

Bella, who was taking a mass of indigestables to Aunt Selina, went to the roof.

"Where is Tom?" Anne asked, as we reached the foot of the stairs. "Gone ahead to fix things," was the answer. But he was not there. At the top of the last flight I stopped, dumb with amazement; the roof had been transformed, enchanted. It was a fairy-land of lights and foliage and colors. I had to stop and rub my eyes. From the bleakness of a tin roof in February to the brightness and greenery of a July roof garden!

"You were the immediate inspiration, Kit," Dallas said. "Harbison thought your headache might come from lack of exercise and fresh air, and he has worked us like nailers all day. I've a blister on my right palm, and Harbison got shocked while he was wiring the place, and nearly fell over the parapet. We bought out two full-sized florists by telephone."

It was the most amazing transformation. At each corner a pole had been erected, and wires crossed the roof diagonally, hung with red and amber bulbs. Around the chimneys had been massed evergreen trees in tubs, hiding their brick-and-mortar ugliness, and among the trees tiny lights were strung. Along the parapet were rows of geometrical boxwood plants in bright red crocks, and the flaps of a crimson and white tent had been thrown open, showing lights within, and rugs, wicker chairs, and cushions.

Max raised a glass of Benedictine and posed for a moment, melodramatically.

"To the Wilson roof garden!" he said. "To Kit, who inspired; to the creators, who perspired; and to Takahiro — may he not have expired."

Everyone was very gay; I think the knowledge that tomorrow Aunt Selina might be with them urged them to make the most of this last night of freedom. I tried to be jolly, and succeeded in being feverish. Mr. Harbison did not come up to enjoy what he had wrought. Jim brought up his guitar and sang love songs in a beautiful tenor, looking at Bella all the time. And Bella sat in a steamer chair, with a rug over her and a spangled veil on her head, looking at the boats on the river — about as soft and as chastened as an an acetylene headlight.

And after Max had told the most improbable tale, which Leila advised him to sprinkle salt on, and Dallas had done a clog dance, Bella said it was time for her complexion sleep and went downstairs, and broke up the party.

"If she only give half as an much care to her immortal soul," Anne said when she had gone, "as she does to her skin, she would let that nice Harbison boy alone. She must have been brutal to him tonight, for he went to bed at nine o'clock. At least, I suppose he went to bed, for he shut himself in the studio, and when I knocked he advised me not to come in."

I had pleaded my headache as an as an excuse for avoiding Aunt Selina all day, and she had not sent for me. Bella was really quite extraordinary. She was never in the habit of putting herself out for anyone, and she always declared that the very odor of a sick room drove her to Scotch and soda. But here she was, rubbing Aunt Selina's back with chloroform liniment — and you know how that smells — getting her up in a chair, dressed in one of Bella's wadded silk robes, with pillows under her feet, and then doing her hair in elaborate puffs — braiding her gray switch and bringing it, coronet-fashion, around the top of her head. She even put rice powder on Aunt Selina's nose, and dabbed violet water behind her ears, and said she couldn't understand why she (Aunt Selina) had never married, but, of course, she probably would some day!

The result was, naturally, that the old lady wouldn't let Bella out of her sight, except to go to the kitchen for something to eat for her. That very day Bella got the doctor to order ale for Aunt Selina (oh, yes; the doctor could come in; Dal said "it was all a-coming in, and nothing going out") and she had three pints of Bass, and learned to eat anchovies and caviar — all in one day.

Bella's conduct to Jim was disgraceful. She snubbed him, ignored him, tramped on him, and Jim was growing positively flabby. He spent most of his time writing letters to the board of health and playing solitaire. He was a pathetic figure.

Well, we went to bed fairly early. Bella had massaged Aunt Selina's face and rubbed in cold cream, Anne and Dallas had compromised on which window should be open in their bedroom, and the men had matched to see who should look at the furnace. I did not expect to sleep, but the cold night air had done its work, and I was asleep almost immediately.

Some time during the early part of the night I wakened, and, after turning and twisting uneasily, I realized that I was cold. The couch in Bella's dressing room was comfortable enough, but narrow and low. I remember distinctly (that was what was so maddening; everybody thought I dreamed it) — I remember getting an eiderdown comfort that was folded at my feet, and pulling it up around me. In the luxury of its warmth I snuggled down and went to sleep almost instantly. It seemed to me I had slept for hours, but it was probably an hour or less, when something roused me. The room was perfectly dark, and there was not a sound save the faint ticking of the clock, but I was wide awake.

And then came the incident that in its ghastly, horrible absurdity made the rest of the people shout with laughter the next day. It was not funny then. For suddenly the eiderdown comfort began to slip. I heard no footstep, not the slightest sound approaching me, but the comfort moved; from my chin, inch by inch, it slipped to my shoulders; awfully, inevitably, hair-raisingly it moved. I could feel my blood gather around my heart, leaving me cold and nerveless. As it passed my hands I gave an involuntary clutch for it, to feel it slip away from my fingers. Then the full horror of the situation took hold of me; as the comfort slid past my feet I sat up and screamed at the top of my voice.

Of course, people came running in all sorts of things. I was still sitting up, declaring I had seen a ghost and that the house was haunted. Dallas was struggling for the second armhole of his dressing gown and Bella had already turned on the lights. They said I had had a nightmare, and not to sleep on my back, and perhaps I was taking grippe.

And just then we heard Jimmy run down the stairs, and fall over something, almost breaking his wrist. It was the eiderdown comfort, half-way up the studio staircase!

Chapter XIII
HE DOES NOT DENY IT

*A*unt Selina got up the next morning and Jim told her all the strange things that had been happening. She fixed on Flannigan, of course, although she still suspected Betty of her watch and other valuables. The incident of the comfort she called nervous indigestion and bad hours.

She spent the entire day going through the storeroom and linen closets, and running her fingers over things for dust. Whenever she found any she looked at me, drew a long breath, and said, "Poor James!" It was maddening. And when she went through his clothes and found some buttons off (Jim didn't keep a man, and Takahiro had stopped at his boots) she looked at me quite awfully.

"His mother was a perfect housekeeper," she said. "James was brought up in clothes with the buttons on, put on clean shelves."

"Didn't they put them on him?" I asked, almost hysterically. It had been a bad morning, after a worse night. Everyone had found fault with the breakfast, and they straggled down one at a time until I was frantic. Then Flannigan had talked to me about the pearls, and Mr. Harbison had said, "Good morning," very stiffly, and nearly rattled the inside of the furnace out.

Early in the morning, too, I overheard a scrap of conversation between the policeman and our gentleman adventurer from South America. Something had gone wrong with the telephone and Mr. Harbison was fussing over it with a screw driver and a pair of scissors — all the tools he could find. Flannigan was lifting rugs to shake them on the roof — Bella's order.

"Wash the table linen!" he was grumbling. "I'll do what I can that's necessary. Grub has to be cooked, and dishes has to be washed — I'll admit that. If you're particular, make up your bed every day; I don't object. But don't tell me we have to use thirty-three table napkins a day. What did folks do before napkins was invented? Tell me that!" — triumphantly.

"What's the answer?" Mr. Harbison inquired absently, evidently with the screw driver in his mouth.

"Used their pocket handkerchiefs! And if the worst comes to the worst, Mr. Harbison, these folks here can use their sleeves, for all I care — not that the women has any sleeves to speak of. Wash clothes I will not."

"Well, don't worry Mrs. Wilson about it," the other voice said. Flannigan straightened himself with a grunt.

"Mrs. Wilson!" he said. "A lot she would worry. She's been a disappointment to me, Mr. Harbison, me thinking that now she'd come back to him, after leavin' him the way she did, they'd be like two turtle doves. Lord! The cook next door —"

But what the cook had told about Bella and Jimmy was not divulged, for the Harbison man caught him up with a jerk and sent Flannigan, grumbling, with his rugs to the roof.

It did not seem possible to carry on the deception much longer, but if things were bad now, what would they be when Aunt Selina learned she had been lied to, made ridiculous, generally deceived? And how would I be able to live in the house with her when she did know? Luckily, everyone was so puzzled over the mystery in the house that numbers of little things that would have been absolutely damning were never noticed at all. For instance, my asking Jimmy at luncheon that day if he took cream in his coffee! And Max coming to the rescue by dropping his watch in his glass of water, and creating a diversion and giving everybody an opportunity to laugh by saying not to mind, it had been in soak before.

Just after luncheon Aunt Selina brought me some undergarments of Jim's to be patched. She explained at length that he had always worn out his undergarments, because he always squirmed around so when he was sitting. And she showed me how to lay one of the garments over a pillow to get the patch in properly.

It was the most humiliating moment of my life, but there was no escape. I took my sewing to the roof, while she went away to find something else for me to do when that was finished, and I sat with the thing on my knee and stared at it, while rebellious tears rolled down my cheeks. The patch was not the shape of the hole at all, and every time I took a stitch I sewed it fast to the pillow beneath. It was terrible. Jim came up after a while and sat down across from me and watched, without saying anything. I suppose what he felt would not have been proper to say to me. We had both reached the point where adequate language failed us. Finally he said:

"I wish I were dead."

"So do I," I retorted, jerking the thread.

"Where is she now?"

"Looking for more of these." I indicated the garment over the pillow, and he wiggled. "Please don't squirm," I said coldly. "You will wear out your — lingerie, and I will have to mend them."

He sat very still for five minutes, when I discovered that I had put the patch in crosswise instead of lengthwise and that it would not fit. As I jerked it out he sneezed.

"Or sneeze," I added venomously. "You will tear your buttons off, and I will have to sew them on."

Jim rose wrathfully. "Don't sit, don't sneeze'," he repeated. "Don't stand, I suppose, for fear I will wear out my socks. Here, give me that. If the fool thing has to be mended, I'll do it myself."

He went over to a corner of the parapet and turned his back to me. He was very much offended. In about a minute he came back, triumphant, and held out the result of his labor. I could only gasp. He had puckered up the edges of the hole like the neck of a bag, and had tied the thread around it. "You — you won't be able to sit down," I ventured.

"Don't have any time to sit," he retorted promptly. "Anyhow, it will give some, won't it? It would if it was tied with elastic instead of thread. Have you any elastic?"

Lollie came up just then, and Jim took himself and his mending downstairs. Luckily, Aunt Selina found several letters in his room that afternoon while she was going over his clothes, and as it took Jim some time to explain them, she forgot the task she had given me altogether.

When Lollie came up to the roof, she closed the door to the stairs, and coming over, drew a chair close to mine.

"Have you seen much of Tom today?" she asked, as an introduction.

"I suppose you mean Mr. Harbison, Lollie," I said. "No — not anymore than I could help. Don't whisper, he couldn't possibly hear you. And if it's scandal I don't want to know it."

"Look here, Kit," she retorted, "you needn't be so superior. If I like to talk scandal, I'm not so sure you aren't making it."

That was the way right along: I was making scandal; I brought them there to dinner; I let Bella in!

And, of course, Anne came up then, and began on me at once.

"You are a very bad girl," she began. "What do you mean by treating Tom Harbison the way you do? He is heart-broken."

"I think you exaggerate my influence over him," I retorted. "I haven't treated him badly, because I haven't paid any attention to him."

Anne threw up her hands.

"There you are!" she said. "He worked all day yesterday fixing this place for you — yes, for you, my dear. I am not blind — and last night you refused to let him bring you up."

"He told you!" I flamed.

"He wondered what he had done. And as you wouldn't let him come within speaking distance of you, he came to me."

"I am sorry, Anne, since you are fond of him," I said. "But to me he is impossible — intolerable. My reasons are quite sufficient."

"Kit is perfectly right, Anne," Leila broke in. "I tell you, there is something queer about him," she added in a portentous whisper.

Anne stiffened.

"He is perfect," she declared. "Of good family, warm-hearted, courageous, handsome, clever — what more do you ask?"

"Honesty," said Leila hotly. "That a man should be what he says he is."

Anne and I both stared.

"It is your Mr. Harbison," Leila went on, "who tried to escape from the house by putting a board across to the next roof!"

"I don't believe it," said Anne. "You might bring me a picture of him, board in hand, and I wouldn't believe it."

"Don't then," Lollie said cruelly. "Let him get away with your pearls; they are yours. Only, as sure as anything, the man who tried to escape from the house had a reason for escaping, and the papers said a man in evening dress and light overcoat. I found Mr. Harbison's overcoat today lying in a heap in one of the maids' rooms, and it was covered with brick dust all over the front. A button had even been torn off."

"Pooh!" Anne said, when she had recovered herself a little. "There isn't any reason, as far as that goes, why Flannigan shouldn't have worn Tom's overcoat, or — any of the others,"

"Flannigan!" Leila said loftily. "Why, his arms are like piano legs; he couldn't get into it. As for the others, there is only one person who would fit, or nearly fit, that overcoat, and that is Dallas, Anne."

While Anne was choking down her wrath, Leila got up and darted out of the tent. When she came back she was triumphant.

"Look," she said, holding out her hand. And on her palm lay a lightish brown button. "I found it just where the paper said the board was thrown out, and it is from Mr. Harbison's overcoat, without a doubt."

Of course I should not have been surprised. A man who would kiss a woman on a dark staircase — a woman he had known only two days — was capable of anything.

"Kit has only been a little keener than the rest of us," Lollie said. "She found him out yesterday."

"Upon my word," said Anne indignantly, preparing to go, "if I didn't know you girls so well, I would think you were crazy. And now, just to offset this, I can tell you something.

Flannigan told me this morning not to worry; that he has my
pearl collar spotted, and that *young ladies will have their jokes!*"

Yes, as I said before, it was a cheerful, joy-producing situation.

I sat and thought it over after Anne's parting shot, when
Leila had flounced downstairs. Things were closing in; I gave
the situation twenty-four hours to develop. At the end of that
time Flannigan would accuse me openly of knowing where
the pearls were; I would explain my silly remark to him and
the mine would explode – under Aunt Selina.

I was sunk in dejected reverie when some one came on the
roof. When he was opposite the opening in the tent, I saw
Mr. Harbison, and at that moment he saw me. He paused
uncertainly, then he made an evident effort and came over
to me.

"You are – better today?"

"Quite well, thank you."

"I am glad you find the tent useful. Does it keep off the
wind?"

"It is quite a shelter" – frigidly.

He still stood, struggling for something to say. Evidently
nothing came to his mind, for he lifted the cap he was
wearing, and turning away, began to work with the wiring of
the roof. He was clever with tools; one could see that. If he
was a professional gentleman-burglar, no doubt he needed to
be. After a bit, finding it necessary to climb to the parapet,
he took off his coat, without even a glance in my direction,
and fell to work vigorously.

One does not need to like a man to admire him physically,
anymore than one needs to like a race horse or any other
splendid animal. No one could deny that the man on the
parapet was a splendid animal; he looked quite big enough
and strong enough to have tossed his slender bridge across
the gulf to the next roof, without any difficulty, and coordi-
nate enough to have crossed on it with a flourish to safety.

Just then there was a rending, tearing sound from the
corner and a muttered ejaculation. I looked up in time to see
Mr. Harbison throw up his arms, make a futile attempt to
regain his balance, and disappear over the edge of the roof.
One instant he was standing there, splendid, superb; the next,

the corner of the parapet was empty, all that stood there was a broken, splintered post and a tangle of wires.

I could not have moved at first; at least, it seemed hours before the full significance of the thing penetrated my dazed brain. When I got up I seemed to walk, to crawl, with leaden weights holding back my feet.

When I got to the corner I had to catch the post for support. I knew somebody was saying, "Oh, how terrible!" over and over. It was only afterward that I knew it had been myself. And then some other voice was saying, "Don't be alarmed. Please don't be frightened. I'm all right."

I dared to look over the parapet, finally, and instead of a crushed and unspeakable body, there was Mr. Harbison, sitting about eight feet below me, with his feet swinging into space and a long red scratch from the corner of his eye across his cheek. There was a sort of mansard there, with windows, and just enough coping to keep him from rolling off.

"I thought you had fallen — all the way," I gasped, trying to keep my lips from trembling. "I — oh, don't dangle your feet like that!"

He did not seem at all glad of his escape. He sat there gloomily, peering into the gulf beneath.

"If it wasn't so — er — messy and generally unpleasant," he replied without looking up, "I would slide off and go the rest of the way."

"You are childish," I said severely. "See if you can get through the window behind you. If you can not, I'll come down and unfasten it." But the window was open, and I had a chance to sit down and gather up the scattered ends of my nerves. To my surprise, however, when he came back he made no effort to renew our conversation. He ignored me completely, and went to work at once to repair the damage to his wires, with his back to me.

"I think you are very rude," I said at last. "You fell over there and I thought you were killed. The nervous shock I experienced is just as bad as if you had gone — all the way."

He put down the hammer and came over to me without speaking. Then, when he was quite close, he said:

"I am very sorry if I startled you. I did not flatter myself that you would be profoundly affected, in any event."

"Oh, as to that," I said lightly, "it makes me ill for days if my car runs over a dog." He looked at me in silence. "You are not going to get up on that parapet again?"

"Mrs. Wilson," he said, without paying the slightest attention to my question, "will you tell me what I have done?"

"Done?"

"Or have not done? I have racked my brains — stayed awake all of last night. At first I hoped it was impersonal, that, womanlike you were merely venting general disfavor on one particular individual. But — your hostility is to me, personally."

I raised my eyebrows, coldly interrogative.

"Perhaps," he went on calmly — "perhaps I was a fool here on the roof — the night before last. If I said anything that I should not, I ask your pardon. If it is not that, I think you ought to ask mine!"

I was angry enough then.

"There can be only one opinion about your conduct," I retorted warmly. "It was worse than brutal. It — it was unspeakable. I have no words for it — except that I loathe it — and you."

He was very grim by this time. "I have heard you say something like that before — only I was not the unfortunate in that case."

"Oh!" I was choking.

"Under different circumstances I should be the last person to recall anything so — personal. But the circumstances are unusual." He took an angry step toward me. "Will you tell me what I have done? Or shall I go down and ask the others?"

"You wouldn't dare," I cried, "or I will tell them what you did! How you waylaid me on those stairs there, and forced your caresses, your kisses, on me! Oh, I could die with shame!"

The silence that followed was as unexpected as it was ominous. I knew he was staring at me, and I was furious to find myself so emotional, so much more the excited of the two. Finally, I looked up.

"You can not deny it," I said, a sort of anti-climax.

"No." He was very quiet, very grim, quite composed. "No," he repeated judicially. "I do not deny it."

He did not? Or he would not? Which?

Chapter XIV

ALMOST, BUT NOT QUITE

Dal had been acting strangely all day. Once, early in the evening, when I had doubled no trump, he led me a club without apology, and later on, during his dummy, I saw him writing our names on the back of an envelope, and putting numbers after them. At my earliest opportunity I went to Max.

"There is something the matter with Dal, Max," I volunteered. "He has been acting strangely all day, and just now he was making out a list — names and numbers."

"You're to blame for that, Kit," Max said seriously. "You put washing soda instead of baking soda in those biscuits today, and he thinks he is a steam laundry. Those are laundry lists he's making out. He asked me a little while ago if I wanted a domestic finish."

Yes, I had put washing soda in the biscuits. The book said soda, and how is one to know which is meant?

"I do not think you are calculated for a domestic finish," I said coldly as I turned away. "In any case I disclaim any such responsibility. But — there is *something* on Dal's mind."

Max came after me. "Don't be cross, Kit. You haven't said a nice word to me today, and you go around bristling with your chin up and two red spots on your cheeks — like whatever-her-name-was with the snakes instead of hair. I don't know why I'm so crazy about you; I always meant to love a girl with a nice disposition."

I left him then. Dal had gone into the reception room and

closed the doors. And because he had been acting so strangely, and partly to escape from Max, whose eyes looked threatening, I followed him. Just as I opened the door quietly and looked in, Dallas switched off the lights, and I could hear him groping his way across the room. Then somebody — not Dal — spoke from the corner, cautiously.

"Is that you, Mr. Brown, sir?" It was Flannigan.

"Yes. Is everything here?"

"All but the powder, sir. Don't step too close. They're spread all over the place."

"Have you taken the curtains down?"

"Yes, sir."

"Matches?"

"Here, sir."

"Light one, will you, Flannigan? I want to see the time."

The flare showed Dallas and Flannigan bent over the timepiece. And it showed something else. The rug had been turned back from the windows which opened on the street, and the curtains had been removed. On the bare hardwood floor just beneath the windows was an array of pans of various sizes, dish pans, cake tins, and a metal foot tub. The pans were raised from the floor on bricks, and seemed to be full of paper. All the chairs and tables were pushed back against the wall, and the bric-a-brac was stacked on the mantel.

"Half an hour yet," Dal said, closing his watch. "Plenty of time, and remember the signal, four short and two long."

"Four short and two long — all right, sir."

"And — Flannigan, here's something for you, on account."

"Thank you, sir."

Dal turned to go out, tripped over the rug, said something, and passed me without an idea of my presence. A moment later Flannigan went out, and I was left, huddled against the wall, and alone.

It was puzzling enough. "Four long and two short!" "All but the powder!" Not that I believed for a moment what Max had said, and anyhow Flannigan was the sanest person I ever saw in my life. But it all seemed a part of the mystery that had been hanging over us for several days. I felt my way across the room and knelt by the pans. Yes, they were there, full of paper and mounted on bricks. It had not been a delusion.

And then I straightened on my knees suddenly, for an automobile passing under the windows had sounded four short honks and two long ones. The signal was followed instantly by a crash. The foot bath had fallen from its supports, and lay, quivering and vibrating with horrid noises at my feet. The next moment Mr. Harbison had thrown open the door and leaped into the room.

"Who's there?" he demanded. Against the light I could see him reaching for his hip pocket, and the rest crowding up around him.

"It's only me," I quavered, "that is, I. The — the dish pan upset."

"Dish pan!" Bella said from back in the crowd. "Kit, of course!"

Jim forced his way through then and turned on the lights. I have no doubt I looked very strange, kneeling there on the bare floor, with a row of pans mounted on bricks behind me, and the furniture all piled on itself in a back corner.

"Kit! What in the world — !" Jim began, and stopped. He stared from me to the pans, to the windows, to the bric-a-brac on the mantel, and back to me.

I sat stonily silent. Why should I explain? Whenever I got into a foolish position, and tried to explain, and tell how it happened, and who was really to blame, they always brought it back to *me* somehow. So I sat there on the floor and let them stare. And finally Lollie Mercer got her breath and said, "How perfectly lovely; it's a charade!"

And Anne guessed "kitchen" at once. "Kit, you know, and the pans and — all that," she said vaguely. At that they all took to guessing! And I sat still, until Mr. Harbison saw the storm in my eyes and came over to me.

"Have you hurt your ankle?" he said in an undertone. "Let me help you up."

"I am not hurt," I said coldly, "and even if I were, it would be unnecessary to trouble you."

"I can not help being troubled," he returned, just as evenly. "'You see, it makes me ill for days if my car runs over a dog.'"

Luckily, at that moment Dal came in. He pushed his way through the crowd without a word, shut off the lights, crashed through the pans and slammed the shutters closed. Then he turned and addressed the rest.

"Of all the lunatics — !" he began, only there was more to it than that. "A fellow goes to all kinds of trouble to put an end to this miserable situation, and the entire household turns out and sets to work to frustrate the whole scheme. You *like* to stay here, don't you, like chickens in a coop? Where's Flannigan?"

Nobody understood Dal's wrath then, but it seems he meant to arrange the plot himself, and when it was ripe, and the hour nearly come, he intended to wager that he could break the quarantine, and to take any odds he could get that he would free the entire party in half an hour. As for the plan itself, it was idiotically simple; we were perfectly delighted when we heard it. It was so simple and yet so comprehensive. We didn't see how it *could* fail. Both the Mercer girls kissed Dal on the strength of it, and Anne was furious. Jim was not so much pleased, for some reason or other, and Mr. Harbison looked thoughtful rather than merry. Aunt Selina had gone to bed.

The idea, of course, was to start an embryo fire just inside the windows, in the pans, to feed it with the orange-fire powder that is used on the Fourth of July, and when we had thrown open the windows and yelled "fire" and all the guards and reporters had rushed to the front of the house, to escape quietly by a rear door from the basement kitchen, get into machines Dal had in waiting, and lose ourselves as quickly as we could.

You can see how simple it was.

We were terribly excited, of course. Everyone rushed madly for motor coats and veils, and Dal shuffled the numbers so the people going the same direction would have the same machine. We called to each other as we dressed about Mamaroneck or Lakewood or wherever we happened to have relatives. Everybody knew everybody else, and his friends. The Mercer girls were going to cruise until the trouble blew over, the Browns were going to Pinehurst, and Jim was going to Africa to hunt, if he could get out of the harbor.

Only the Harbison man seemed to have no plans; quite suddenly with the world so near again, the world of country houses and steam yachts and all the rest of it, he ceased to be

one of us. It was not his world at all. He stood back and
watched the kaleidoscope of our coats and veils, half-quizzi-
cally, but with something in his face that I had not seen there
before. If he had not been so self-reliant and big, I would have
said he was lonely. Not that he was pathetic in any sense of
the word. Of course, he avoided me, which was natural and
exactly what I wished. Bella never was far from him and at
the last she loaded him with her jewel case and a muff and
traveling bag and asked him to her cousins' on Long Island.
I felt sure he was going to decline, when he glanced across at
me.

"Do go," I said, very politely. "They are charming people."
And he accepted at once!

It was a transparent plot on Bella's part: Two elderly
maiden ladies, house miles from anywhere, long evenings in
the music room with an open fire and Bella at the harp
playing the two songs she knows.

When we were ready and gathered in the kitchen, in the
darkness, of course, Dal went up on the roof and signaled
with a lantern to the cars on the drive. Then he went downstairs, took a last look at the drawing room, fired the papers,
shook on the powder, opened the windows and yelled "fire!"

Of course, huddled in the kitchen we had heard little or
nothing. But we plainly heard Dal on the first floor and
Flannigan on the second yelling "fire," and the patter of feet
as the guards ran to the front of the house. And at that instant
we remembered Aunt Selina!

That was the cause of the whole trouble. I don't know why
they turned on me; she wasn't my aunt. But by the time we
had got her out of bed, and had wrapped her in an eiderdown
comfort, and stuck slippers on her feet and a motor veil on
her head, the glare at the front of the house was beginning
to die away. She didn't understand at all and we had no time
to explain. I remember that she wanted to go back and get
her "plate," whatever that may be, but Jim took her by the
arm and hurried her along, and the rest, who had waited, and
were in awful tempers, stood aside and let them out first.

The door to the area steps was open, and by the street lights
we could see a fence and a gate, which opened on a side street.
Jim and Aunt Selina ran straight for the gate; the wind

blowing Aunt Selina's comfort like a sail. Then, with our feet, so to speak, on the first rungs of the ladder of Liberty, it slipped. A half-dozen guards and reporters came around the house and drove us back like sheep into a slaughter pen. It was the most humiliating moment of my life.

Dal had been for fighting a way through, and just for a minute I think I went Berserk myself. But Max spied one of the reporters setting up a flash light as we stood, undecided, at the top of the steps, and after that there was nothing to do but retreat. We backed down slowly, to show them we were not afraid. And when we were all in the kitchen again, and had turned on the lights and Bella was crying with her head against Mr. Harbison's arm, Dal said cheerfully,

"Well, it has done some good, anyhow. We have lost Aunt Selina."

And we all shook hands on it, although we were sorry about Jim. And Dal said we would have some champagne and drink to Aunt Selina's comfort, and we could have her teeth fumigated and send them to her. Somebody said "Poor old Jim," and at that Bella looked up.

She stared around the group, and then she went quite pale.

"Jim!" she gasped. "Do you mean — that Jim is — out there too?"

"Jim and Aunt Selina!" I said as calmly as I could for joy. You can see how it simplified the situation for me. "By this time they are a mile away, and going!"

Everybody shook hands again except Bella. She had dropped into a chair, and sat biting her lip and breathing hard, and she would not join in any of the hilarity at getting rid of Aunt Selina. Finally she got up and knocked over her chair.

"You are a lot of cowards," she stormed. "You deserted them out there, left them. Heaven knows where they are — a defenseless old woman, and — and a man who did not even have an overcoat. And it is snowing!"

"Never mind," Dal said reassuringly. "He can borrow Aunt Selina's comfort. Make the old lady discard from weakness. Anyhow, Bella, if I know anything of human nature, the old lady will make it hot enough for him. Poor old Jim!"

Then they shook hands again, and with that there came a

terrible banging at the door, which we had locked.

"Open the door!" some one commanded. It was one of the guards.

"Open it yourself!" Dallas called, moving a kitchen table to reinforce the lock.

"Open that door or we will break it in!"

Dallas put his hands in his pockets, seated himself on the table, and whistled cheerfully. We could hear them conferring outside, and they made another appeal which was refused. Suddenly Bella came over and confronted Dallas.

"They have brought them back!" she said dramatically. "They are out there now; I distinctly heard Jim's voice. Open that door, Dallas!"

"Oh, *don't* let them in!" I wailed. It was quite involuntary, but the disappointment was too awful. "Dallas, *don't* open that door!"

Dal swung his feet and smiled from Bella to me.

"Think what a solution it is to all our difficulties," he said easily. "Without Aunt Selina I could be happy here indefinitely."

There was more knocking, and somebody — Max, I think — said to let them in, that it was a fool thing anyhow, and that he wanted to go to bed and forget it; his feet were cold. And just then there was a crash, and part of one of the windows fell in. The next blow from outside brought the rest of the glass, and — somebody was coming through, feet first. It was Jim.

He did not speak to any of us, but turned and helped in a bundle of red and yellow silk comfort that proved to be Aunt Selina, also feet first. I had a glimpse of a half-dozen heads outside, guards and reporters. Then Jim jerked the shade down and unswathed Aunt Selina's legs so that she could walk, offered his arm, and stalked past us and upstairs, without a word!

None of us spoke. We turned out the lights and went upstairs and took off our wraps and went to bed. It had been almost a fiasco.

Chapter XV

SUSPICION AND DISCORD

*E*veryone was nasty the next morning. Aunt Selina declared that her feet were frost-bitten and kept Bella rubbing them with ice water all morning. And Jim was impossible. He refused to speak to any of us and he watched Bella furtively, as if he suspected her of trying to get him out of the house.

When luncheon time came around and he had shown no indication of going to the telephone and ordering it, we had a conclave, and Max was chosen to remind him of the hour. Jim was shut in the studio, and we waited together in the hall while Max went up. When he came down he was somewhat ruffled.

"He wouldn't open the door," he reported, "and when I told him it was meal time, he said he wasn't hungry, and he didn't give a whoop about the rest of us. He had asked us here to dinner; he hadn't proposed to adopt us."

So we finally ordered luncheon ourselves, and about two o'clock Jim came downstairs sheepishly, and ate what was left. Anne declared that Bella had been scolding him in the upper hall, but I doubted it. She was never seen to speak to him unnecessarily.

The excitement of the escape over, Mr. Harbison and I remained on terms of armed neutrality. And Max still hunted for Anne's pearls, using them, the men declared, as a good excuse to avoid tinkering with the furnace or repairing the dumb waiter, which took the queerest notions, and stopped once, half-way up from the kitchen, for an hour, with the

dinner on it. Anyhow, Max was searching the house systematically, armed with a copy of Poe's Purloined Letter and
Gaboriau's Monsieur LeCoq. He went through the seats of
the chairs with hatpins, tore up the beds, and lifted rugs, until
the house was in a state of confusion. And the next day, the
fourth, he found something — not much, but it was curious.
He had been in the studio, poking around behind the dusty
pictures, with Jimmy expostulating every time he moved
anything and the rest standing around watching him.

Max was strutting.

"We get it by elimination," he said importantly. "The pearls
being nowhere else in the house, they must be here in the
studio. Three parts of the studio having yielded nothing, they
must be in the fourth. Ladies and gentlemen, let me have
your attention for one moment. I tap this canvas with my
wand — there is nothing up my sleeve. Then I prepare to move
the canvas — so. And I put my hand in the pocket of this
disreputable velvet coat, so. Behold!"

Then he gave a low exclamation and looked at something
he held in his hand. Everyone stepped forward, and on his
palm was the small diamond clasp from Anne's collar!

Jimmy was apoplectic. He tried to smile, but no one else
did.

"Well, I'll be flabbergasted!" he said. "I say, you people, you
don't think for a minute that I put that thing there? Why, I
haven't worn that coat for a month. It's — it's a trick of yours,
Max."

But Max shook his head; he looked stupefied, and stood
gazing from the clasp to the pocket of the old painting coat.
Betty dropped on a folding stool, that promptly collapsed
with her and created a welcome diversion, while Anne
pounced on the clasp greedily, with a little cry.

"We will find it all now," she said excitedly. "Did you look
in the other pockets, Max?"

Then, for the first time, I was conscious of an air of
constraint among the men. Dallas was whistling softly, and
Mr. Harbison, having rescued Betty, was standing silent and
aloof, watching the scene with non-committal eyes. It was
Max who spoke first, after a hurried inventory of the other
pockets.

"Nothing else," he said constrainedly. "I'll move the rest of the canvases."

But Jim interfered, to everyone's surprise.

"I wouldn't, if I were you, Max. There's nothing back there. I had 'em out yesterday." He was quite pale.

"Nonsense!" Max said gruffly. "If it's a practical joke, Jim, why don't you fess up? Anne has worried enough."

"The pearls are not there, I tell you," Jim began. Although the studio was cold, there were little fine beads of moisture on his face. "I must ask you not to move those pictures." And then Aunt Selina came to the rescue; she stalked over and stood with her back against the stack of canvases.

"As far as I can understand this," she declaimed, "you gentlemen are trying to intimate that James knows something of that young woman's jewelry, because you found part of it in his pocket. Certainly you will not move the pictures. How do you know that the young gentleman who said he found it there didn't have it up his sleeve?"

She looked around triumphantly, and Max glowered. Dallas soothed her, however.

"Exactly so," he said. "How do we know that Max didn't have the clasp up his sleeve? My dear lady, neither my wife nor I care anything for the pearls, as compared with the priceless pearl of peace. I suggest tea on the roof; those in favor — ? My arm, Miss Caruthers."

It was all well enough for Jim to say later that he didn't dare to have the canvases moved, for he had stuck behind them all sorts of chorus girl photographs and life-class crayons that were not for Aunt Selina's eye, besides four empty siphons, two full ones, and three bottles of whisky. Not a soul believed him; there was a new element of suspicion and discord in the house.

Everyone went up on the roof and left him to his mystery. Anne drank her tea in a preoccupied silence, with half-closed eyes, an attitude that boded ill to somebody. The rest were feverishly gay, and Aunt Selina, with a pair of arctics on her feet and a hot-water bottle at her back, sat in the middle of the tent and told me familiar anecdotes of Jimmy's early youth (had he known, he would have slain her). Betty and Mr. Harbison had found a medicine ball, and were running around like a pair of children. It was quite certain that neither his escape from death nor my accusation weighed heavily on him.

While Aunt Selina was busy with the time Jim had swallowed an open safety pin, and just as the pin had been coughed up, or taken out of his nose — I forget which — Jim himself appeared and sulkily demanded the privacy of the roof for his training hour.

Yes, he was training. Flannigan claimed to know the system that had reduced the president to what he is, and he and Jim had a séance every day which left Jim feeling himself for bruises all evening. He claimed to be losing flesh; he said he could actually feel it going, and he and Flannigan had spent an entire afternoon in the cellar three days before with a potato barrel, a cane-seated chair and a lamp.

The whole thing had been shrouded in mystery. They sandpapered the inside of the barrel and took out all the nails, and when they had finished they carried it to the roof and put it in a corner behind the tent. Everybody was curious, but Flannigan refused any information about it, and merely said it was part of his system. Dal said that if *he* had anything like that in his system he certainly would be glad to get rid of it.

At a quarter to six Jim appeared, still sullen from the events of the afternoon and wearing a dressing gown and a pair of slippers, Flannigan following him with a sponge, a bucket of water and an armful of bath towels. Everybody protested at having to move, but he was firm, and they all filed down the stairs. I was the last, with Aunt Selina just ahead of me. At the top of the stairs, she turned around suddenly to me.

"That policeman looks cruel," she said. "What's more, he's been in a bad humor all day. More than likely he'll put James flat on the roof and tramp on him, under pretense of training him. All policemen are inhuman."

"He only rolls him over a barrel or something like that," I protested.

"James had a bump like an egg over his ear last night," Aunt Selina insisted, glaring at Flannigan's unconscious back. "I don't think it's safe to leave him. It is my time to relax for thirty minutes, or I would watch him. You will have to stay," she said, fixing me with her imperious eyes.

So I stayed. Jim didn't want me, and Flannigan muttered mutiny. But it was easier to obey Aunt Selina than to clash with her, and anyhow I wanted to see the barrel in use.

I never saw anyone train before. It is not a joyful spectacle. First, Flannigan made Jim run, around and around the roof. He said it stirred up his food and brought it in contact with his liver, to be digested.

Flannigan, from meekness and submission, of a sort, in the kitchen, became an autocrat on the roof.

"Once more," he would say. "Pick up your feet, sir! Pick up your feet!"

And Jim would stagger doggedly past me, where I sat on the parapet, his poor cheeks shaking and the tail of his bath robe wrapping itself around his legs. Yes, he ran in the bath robe in deference to me. It seems there isn't much to a running suit.

"Head up," Flannigan would say. "Lift your knees, sir. Didn't you ever see a horse with string halt?"

He let him stop finally, and gave him a moment to get his breath. Then he set him to turning somersaults. They spread the cushions from the couch in the tent on the roof, and Jim would poke his head down and say a prayer, and then curve over as gracefully as a sausage and come up gasping, as if he had been pushed off a boat.

"Five pounds a day; not less, sir," Flannigan said encouragingly. "You'll drop it in chunks."

Jim looked at the tin as if he expected to see the chunks lying at his feet.

"Yes," he said, wiping the back of his neck. "If we're in here thirty days that will be one hundred and fifty pounds. Don't forget to stop in time, Flannigan. I don't want to melt away like a candle."

He was cheered, however, by the promise of reduction.

"What do you think of that, Kit?" he called to me. "Your uncle is going to look as angular as a problem in geometry. I'll — I'll be the original *reductio ad absurdum.* Do you want me to stand on my head, Flannigan? Wouldn't that reduce something?"

"Your brains, sir," Flannigan retorted gravely, and presented a pair of boxing gloves. Jim visibly quailed, but he put them on.

"Do you know, Flannigan," he remarked, as he fastened them, "I'm thinking of wearing these all the time. They hide my character."

Flannigan looked puzzled, but he did not ask an explanation. He demanded that Jim shed the bath robe, which he finally did, on my promise to watch the sunset. Then for fully a minute there was no sound save of feet running rapidly around the roof, and an occasional soft thud. Each thud was accompanied by a grunt or two from Jim. Flannigan was grimly silent. Once there was a smart rap, an oath from the policeman, and a mirthless chuckle from Jim. The chuckle ended in a crash, however, and I turned. Jim was lying on his back on the roof, and Flannigan was wiping his ear with a towel. Jim sat up and ran his hand down his ribs.

"They're all here," he observed after a minute. "I thought I missed one."

"The only way to take a man's weight down," Flannigan said dryly.

Jim got up dizzily.

"Down on the roof, I suppose you mean," he said.

The next proceedings were mysterious. Flannigan rolled the barrel into the tent, and carried in a small glass lamp. With the material at hand he seemed to be effecting a combination, no new one, to judge by his facility. Then he called Jim.

At the door of the tent Jim turned to me, his bathrobe toga fashion around his shoulders.

"This is a very essential part of the treatment," he said solemnly. "The exercise, according to Flannigan, loosens up the adipose tissue. The next step is to boil it out. I hope, unless your instructions compel you, that you will at least have the decency to stay out of the tent."

"I am going at once," I said, outraged. "I'm not here because I'm mad about it, and you know it. And don't pose with that bath robe. If you think you're a character out of Roman history, look at your legs."

"I didn't mean to offend you," he said sulkily. "Only I'm tired of having you choked down my throat every time I open my mouth, Kit. And don't go just yet. Flannigan is going for my clothes as soon as he lights the — the lamp, and — somebody ought to watch the stairs."

That was all there was to it. I said I would guard the steps, and Flannigan, having ignited the combination, whatever it was, went downstairs. How was I to know that Bella would come up when she did? Was it my fault that the lamp got too high, and that Flannigan couldn't hear Jim calling? Or that just as Bella reached the top of the steps Jim should come to the door of the tent, wearing the barrel part of his hot-air cabinet, and yelling for a doctor?

Bella came to a dead stop on the upper step, with her mouth open. She looked at Jim, at the inadequate barrel, and from them she looked at me. Then she began to laugh, one of her hysterical giggles, and she turned and went down again. As Jim and I stared at each other we could hear her gurgling down the hall below.

She had violent hysterics for an hour, with Anne rubbing her forehead and Aunt Selina burning a feather out of the feather duster under her nose. Only Jim and I understood, and we did not tell. Luckily, the next thing that occurred drove Bella and her nerves from everybody's mind.

At seven o'clock, when Bella had dropped asleep and everybody else was dressed for dinner, Aunt Selina discovered that the house was cold, and ordered Dal to the furnace.

It was Dal's day at the furnace; Flannigan had been relieved of that part of the work after twice setting fire to a chimney.

In five minutes Dal came back and spoke a few words to Max, who followed him to the basement, and in ten minutes more Flannigan puffed up the steps and called Mr. Harbison.

I am not curious, but I knew that something had happened. While Aunt Selina was talking suffrage to Anne — who said she had always been tremendously interested in the subject, and if women got the suffrage would they be allowed to vote? — I slipped back to the dining room.

The table was laid for dinner, but Flannigan was not in sight. I could hear voices from somewhere, faint voices that talked rapidly, and after a while I located the sounds under my feet. The men were all in the basement, and something must have happened. I flew back to the basement stairs, to meet Mr. Harbison at the foot. He was grimy and dusty, with streaks of coal dust over his face, and he had been examining his revolver. I was just in time to see him slip it into his pocket.

"What is the matter?" I demanded. "Is anyone hurt?

"No one," he said coolly. "We've been cleaning out the furnace."

"With a revolver! How interesting — and unusual!" I said dryly, and slipped past him as he barred the way. He was not pleased; I heard him mutter something and come rapidly after me, but I had the voices as a guide, and I was not going to be turned back like a child. The men had gathered around a low stone arch in the furnace room, and were looking down a short flight of steps, into a sort of vault, evidently under the pavement. A faint light came from a small grating above, and there was a close, musty smell in the air.

"I tell you it must have been last night," Dallas was saying. "Wilson and I were here before we went to bed, and I'll swear that hole was not there then."

"It was not there this morning, sir," Flannigan insisted. "It has been made during the day."

"And it could not have been done this afternoon," Mr. Harbison said quietly. "I was fussing with the telephone wire down here. I would have heard the noise."

Something in his voice made me look at him, and certainly his expression was unusual. He was watching us all intently while Dallas pointed out to me the cause of the excitement. From the main floor of the furnace room, a flight of stone steps surmounted by an arch led into the coal cellar, beneath the street. The coal cellar was of brick, with a cement floor, and in the left wall there gaped an opening about three feet by three, leading into a cavernous void, perfectly black — evidently a similar vault belonging to the next house.

The whole place was ghostly, full of shadows, shivery with possibilities. It was Mr. Harbison finally who took Jim's candle and crawled through the aperture. We waited in dead silence, listening to his feet crunching over the coal beyond, watching the faint yellow light that came through the ragged opening in the wall. Then he came back and called through to us.

"Place is locked, over here," he said. "Heavy oak door at the head of the steps. Whoever made that opening has done a prodigious amount of labor for nothing."

The weapon, a crowbar, lay on the ground beside the bricks, and he picked it up and balanced it on his hand. Dallas' florid face was almost comical in his bewilderment; as for Jimmy — he slammed a piece of slag at the furnace and walked away. At the door he turned around.

"Why don't you accuse me of it?" he asked bitterly. "Maybe you could find a lump of coal in my pockets if you searched me."

He stalked up the stairs then and left us. Dallas and I went up together, but we did not talk. There seemed to be nothing to say. Not until I had closed and locked the door of my room did I venture to look at something that I carried in the palm of my hand. It was a watch, not running — a gentleman's flat gold watch, and it had been hanging by its fob to a nail in the bricks beside the aperture.

In the back of the watch were the initials, T.H.H. and the picture of a girl, cut from a newspaper.

It was my picture.

Chapter XVI
I FACE FLANNIGAN

*D*inner waited that night while everybody went to the coal cellar and stared at the hole in the wall, and watched while Max took a tracing of it and of some footprints in the coal dust on the other side.

I did not go. I went into the library with the guilty watch in the fold of my gown, and found Mr. Harbison there, staring through the February gloom at the blank wall of the next house, and quite unconscious of the reporter with a drawing pad just below him in the area-way. I went over and closed the shutters before his very eyes, but even then he did not move.

"Will you be good enough to turn around?" I demanded at last.

"Oh!" he said wheeling. "Are *you* here?"

There wasn't any reply to that, so I took the watch and placed it on the library table between us. The effect was all that I had hoped. He stared at it for an instant, then at me, and with his hand outstretched for it, stopped.

"Where did you find it?" he asked. I couldn't understand his expression. He looked embarrassed, but not at all afraid.

"I think you know, Mr. Harbison," I retorted.

"I wish I did. You opened it?"

"Yes."

We stood looking at each other across the table. It was his glance that wavered.

"About the picture – of you," he said at last. "You see,

down there in South America, a fellow hasn't much to do in
the evenings, and a — a chum of mine and I — we were awfully
down on what we called the plutocrats, the — the leisure
classes. And when that picture of yours came in the paper,
we had — we had an argument. He said —" He stopped.

"What did he say?"

"Well, he said it was the picture of an empty-faced society
girl."

"Oh!" I exclaimed.

"I — I maintained there were possibilities in the face." He
put both hands on the table, and, bending forward, looked
down at me. "Well, I was a fool, I admit. I said your eyes were
kind and candid, in spite of that haughty mouth. You see, I
said I was a fool."

"I think you are exceedingly rude," I managed finally. "If
you want to know where I found your watch, it was down in
the coal cellar. And if you admit you are an idiot, I am not.
I — I know all about Bella's bracelet — and the board on the
roof, and — oh, if you would only leave — Anne's necklace —
on the coal, or somewhere — and get away —"

My voice got beyond me then, and I dropped into a chair
and covered my face. I could feel him staring at the back of
my head.

"Well, I'll be —" something or other, he said finally, and
then he turned on his heel and went out. By the time I got
my eyes dry (yes, I was crying; I always do when I am angry)
I heard Jim coming downstairs, and I tucked the watch out
of sight. Would anyone have foreseen the trouble that watch
would make!

Jim was sulky. He dropped into a chair and stretched out
his legs, looking gloomily at nothing. Then he got up and
ambled into his den, closing the door behind him without
having spoken a word. It was more than human nature could
stand.

When I went into the den he was stretched on the daven-
port with his face buried in the cushions. He looked absolutely wilted, and every line of him was drooping.

"Go on out, Kit," he said, in a smothered voice. "Be a good
girl and don't follow me around."

"You are shameless!" I gasped. "Follow you! When you are

hung around my neck like a — like a —" Millstone was what I wanted to say, but I couldn't think of it.

He turned over and looked up from his cushions like an ill-treated and suffering cherub.

"I'm done for, Kit," he groaned. "Bella went up to the studio after we left, and investigated that corner."

"What did she find? The necklace?" I asked eagerly. He was too wretched to notice this.

"No, that picture of you that I did last winter. She is crazy — she says she is going upstairs and sit in Takahiro's room and take smallpox and die."

"Fiddlesticks!" I said rudely, and somebody hammered on the door and opened it.

"Pardon me for disturbing you," Bella said, in her best dear-me-I'm-glad-I-knocked manner. "But — Flannigan says the dinner has not come."

"Good Lord!" Jim exclaimed. "I forgot to order the confounded dinner!"

It was eight o'clock by that time, and as it took an hour at least after telephoning the order, everybody looked blank when they heard. The entire family, except Mr. Harbison, who had not appeared again, escorted Jim to the telephone and hung around hungrily, suggesting new dishes every minute. And then — he couldn't raise Central. It was fifteen minutes before we gave up, and stood staring at one another despairingly.

"Call out of a window, and get one of those infernal reporters to do something useful for once," Max suggested. But he was indignantly hushed. We would have starved first. Jim was peering into the transmitter and knocking the receiver against his hand, like a watch that had stopped. But nothing happened. Flannigan reported a box of breakfast food, two lemons, and a pineapple cheese, a combination that didn't seem to lend itself to anything.

We went back to the dining room from sheer force of habit and sat around the table and looked at the lemonade Flannigan had made. Anne *would* talk about the salad her last cook had concocted, and Max told about a little town in Connecticut where the restaurant keeper smokes a corn-cob pipe while he cooks the most luscious fried clams in America. And Aunt

Selina related that in her family they had a recipe for chicken smothered in cream. And then we sipped the weak lemonade and nibbled at the cheese.

"To change this gridiron martyrdom," Dallas said finally, "where's Harbison? Still looking for his watch?"

"Watch!" Everybody said it in a different tone.

"Sure," he responded. "Says his watch was taken last night from the studio. Better get him down to take a squint at the telephone. Likely he can fix it."

Flannigan was beside me with the cheese. And at that moment I felt Mr. Harbison's stolen watch slip out of my girdle, slide greasily across my lap, and clatter to the floor. Flannigan stooped, but luckily it had gone under the table. To have had it picked up, to have had to explain how I got it, to see them try to ignore my picture pasted in it — oh, it was impossible! I put my foot over it.

"Drop something?" Dallas asked perfunctorily, rising. Flannigan was still half kneeling.

"A fork," I said, as easily as I could, and the conversation went on. But Flannigan knew, and I knew he knew. He watched my every movement like a hawk after that, standing just behind my chair. I dropped my useless napkin, to have it whirled up before it reached the floor. I said to Betty that my shoe buckle was loose, and actually got the watch in my hand, only to let it slip at the critical moment. Then they all got up and went sadly back to the library, and Flannigan and I faced each other.

Flannigan was not a handsome man at any time, though up to then he had at least looked amiable. But now as I stood with my hand on the back of my chair, his face grew suddenly menacing. The silence was absolute. I was the guiltiest wretch alive, and opposite me the law towered and glowered, and held the yellow remnant of a pineapple cheese! And in the silence that wretched watch lay and ticked and ticked and ticked. Then Flannigan creaked over and closed the door into the hall, came back, picked up the watch, and looked at it.

"You're unlucky, I'm thinkin'," he said finally. "You've got the nerve all right, but you ain't cute enough."

"I don't know what you mean," I quavered. "Give me that watch to return to Mr. Harbison."

"Not on your life," he retorted easily. "I give it back myself, like I did the bracelet, and — like I'm going to give back the necklace, if you'll act like a sensible little girl."

I could only choke.

"It's foolish, any way you look at it," he persisted. "here you are, lots of friends, folks that think you're all right. Why, I reckon there isn't one of them that wouldn't lend you money if you needed it so bad."

"Will you be still?" I said furiously. "Mr. Harbison left that watch — with me — an hour ago. Get him, and he will tell you so himself!"

"Of course he would," Flannigan conceded, looking at me with grudging approval. "He wouldn't be what I think he is, if he didn't lie up and down for you." There were voices in the hall. Flannigan came closer. "An hour ago, you say. And he told me it was gone this morning! It's a losing game, miss. I'll give you twenty-four hours and then — the necklace, if you please, miss."

Chapter XVII
A CLASH AND A KISS

*T*he clash that came that evening had been threatening for some time. Take an immovable body, represented by Mr. Harbison and his square jaw, and an irresistible force, Jimmy and his weight, and there is bound to be trouble.

The real fault was Jim's. He had gone entirely mad again over Bella, and thrown prudence to the winds. He mooned at her across the dinner table, and waylaid her on the stairs or in the back halls, just to hear her voice when she ordered him out of her way. He telephoned for flowers and candy for her quite shamelessly, and he got out a book of photographs that they had taken on their wedding journey, and kept it on the library table. The sole concession he made to our presumptive relationship was to bring me the responsibility for everything that went wrong, and his shirts for buttons.

The first I heard of the trouble was from Dal. He waylaid me in the hall after dinner that night, and his face was serious.

"I'm afraid we can't keep it up very long, Kit," he said. "With Jim trailing Bella all over the house, and the old lady keener every day, it's bound to come out somehow. And that isn't all. Jim and Harbison had a set-to today — about you."

"About me!" I repeated. "Oh, I dare say I have been falling short again. What was Jim doing? Abusing me?"

Dal looked cautiously over his shoulder, but no one was near.

"It seems that the gentle Bella has been unusually beastly today to Jim, and — I believe she's jealous of you, Kit. Jim followed her up to the roof before dinner with a box of flowers, and she tossed them over the parapet. She said, I believe, that she didn't want his flowers; he could buy them for you, and be damned to him, or some ladylike equivalent."

"Jim is a jellyfish," I said contemptuously. "What did he say?"

"He said he only cared for one woman, and that was Bella; that he never had really cared for you and never would, and that divorce courts were not unmitigated evils if they showed people the way to real happiness. Which wouldn't amount to anything if Harbison had not been in the tent, trying to sleep!"

Dal did not know all the particulars, but it seems that relations between Jim and Mr. Harbison were rather strained. Bella had left the roof and Jim and the Harbison man came face to face in the door of the tent. According to Dal, little had been said, but Jim, bound by his promise to me, could not explain, and could only stammer something about being an old friend of Miss Knowles. And Tom had replied shortly that it was none of his business, but that there were some things friendship hardly justified, and tried to pass Jim. Jim was instantly enraged; he blocked the door to the roof and demanded to know what the other man meant. There were two or three versions of the answer he got. The general purport was that Mr. Harbison had no desire to explain further, and that the situation was forced on him. But if he insisted — when a man systematically ignored and neglected his wife for some one else, there were communities where he would be tarred and feathered.

"Meaning me?" Jim demanded, apoplectic.

"The remark was a general one," Mr. Harbison retorted, "but if you wish to make a concrete application — !"

Dal had gone up just then, and found them glaring at each other, Jim with his hands clenched at his sides, and Mr. Harbison with his arms folded and very erect. Dal took Jim by the elbow and led him downstairs, muttering, and the situation was saved for the time. But Dal was not optimistic.

"You can do a bit yourself, Kit," he finished. "Look more cheerful, flirt a little. You can do that without trying. Take Max on for a day or so; it would be charity anyhow. But don't let Tom Harbison take into his head that you are grieving over Jim's neglect, or he's likely to toss him off the roof."

"I have no reason to think that Mr. Harbison cares one way or the other about me," I said primly. "You don't think he's — he's in love with me, do you, Dal?" I watched him out of the corner of my eye, but he only looked amused.

"In love with you!" he repeated. "Why bless your wicked little heart, no! He thinks you're a married woman! It's the principle of the thing he's fighting for. If I had as much principle as he has, I'd — I'd put it out at interest."

Max interrupted us just then, and asked if we knew where Mr. Harbison was.

"Can't find him," he said. "I've got the telephone together and have enough left over to make another. Where do you suppose Harbison hides the tools? I'm working with a corkscrew and two palette knives."

I heard nothing more of the trouble that night. Max went to Jim about it, and Jim said angrily that only a fool would interfere between a man and his wife — wives. Whereupon Max retorted that a fool and his wives were soon parted, and left him. The two principals were coldly civil to each other, and smaller issues were lost as the famine grew more and more insistent. For famine it was.

They worked the rest of the evening, but the telephone refused to revive and everyone was starving. Individually our pride was at low ebb, but collectively it was still formidable. So we sat around and Jim played Grieg with the soft stops on, and Aunt Selina went to bed. The weather had changed, and it was sleeting, but anything was better than the drawing room. I was in a mood to battle with the elements or to cry — or both — so I slipped out, while Dal was reciting "Give me three grains of corn, mother," threw somebody's overcoat over my shoulders, put on a man's soft hat — Jim's I think — and went up to the roof.

It was dark in the third floor hall, and I had to feel my way to the foot of the stairs. I went up quietly, and turned the knob of the door to the roof. At first it would not open, and I could hear the wind howling outside. Finally, however, I got the door open a little and wormed my way through. It was not entirely dark out there, in spite of the storm. A faint reflection of the street lights made it possible to distinguish the outlines of the boxwood plants, swaying in the wind, and the chimneys and the tent. And then — a dark figure disentangled itself from the nearest chimney and seemed to hurl itself at me. I remember putting out my hands and trying to say something, but the figure caught me roughly by the shoulders and knocked me back against the door frame. From miles away a heavy voice was saying, "So I've got you!" and then the roof gave from under me, and I was floating out on the storm, and sleet was beating in my face, and the wind was whispering over and over, "Open your eyes, for God's sake!"

I did open them after a while, and finally I made out that I was laying on the floor in the tent. The lights were on, and I had a cold and damp feeling, and something wet was trickling down my neck.

I seemed to be alone, but in a second somebody came into the tent, and I saw it was Mr. Harbison, and that he had a double handful of half-melted snow. He looked frantic and determined, and only my sitting up quickly prevented my getting another snow bath. My neck felt queer and stiff, and I was very dizzy. When he saw that I was conscious he dropped the snow and stood looking down at me.

"Do you know," he said grimly, "that I very nearly choked you to death a little while ago?"

"It wouldn't surprise me to be told so," I said. "Do I know too much, or what is it, Mr. Harbison?" I felt terribly ill, but I would not let him see it. "It is queer, isn't it — how we always select the roof for our little — differences?" He seemed to relax somewhat at my gibe.

"I didn't know it was you," he explained shortly. "I was waiting for — some one, and in the hat you wore and the coat, I mistook you. That's all. Can you stand?"

"No," I retorted. I could, but his summary manner displeased me. The sequel, however, was rather amazing, for he stooped suddenly and picked me up, and the next instant we were out in the storm together. At the door he stooped and felt for the knob.

"Turn it," he commanded. "I can't reach it."

"I'll do nothing of the kind," I said shrewishly. "Let me down; I can walk perfectly well."

He hesitated. Then he slid me slowly to my feet, but he did not open the door at once. "Are you afraid to let me carry you down those stairs, after — Tuesday night?" he asked, very low. "You still think I did that?"

I had never been less sure of it than at that moment, but an imp of perversity made me retort, "Yes."

He hardly seemed to hear me. He stood looking down at me as I leaned against the door frame.

"Good Lord!" he groaned. "To think that I might have killed you!" And then — he stooped and suddenly kissed me.

The next moment the door was open, and he was leading me down into the house. At the foot of the staircase he paused, still holding my hand, and faced me in the darkness.

"I'm not sorry," he said steadily. "I suppose I ought to be, but I'm not. Only — I want you to know that I was not guilty — before. I didn't intend to now. I am — almost as much surprised as you are."

I was quite unable to speak, but I wrenched my hand loose. He stepped back to let me pass, and I went down the hall alone.

Chapter XVIII
IT'S ALL MY FAULT

I didn't go to the drawing room again. I went into my own room and sat in the dark, and tried to be furiously angry, and only succeeded in feeling queer and tingly. One thing was absolutely certain: not the same man, but two different men had kissed me on the stairs to the roof. It sounds rather horrid and discriminating, but there was all the difference in the world.

But then — who had? And for whom had Mr. Harbison been waiting on the roof? "Did you know that I nearly choked you to death a few minutes ago?" Then he rather expected to finish somebody in that way! Who? Jim, probably. It was strange, too, but suddenly I realized that no matter how many suspicious things I mustered up against him — and there were plenty — down in my heart I didn't believe him guilty of anything, except this last and unforgivable offense. Whoever was trying to leave the house had taken the necklace, that seemed clear, unless Max was still foolishly trying to break quarantine and create one of the sensations he so dearly loves. This was a new idea, and some things upheld it, but Max had been playing bridge when I was kissed on the stairs, and there was still left that ridiculous incident of the comfort.

Bella came up after I had gone to bed, and turned on the light to brush her hair.

"If I don't leave this mausoleum soon, I'll be carried out," she declared. "You in bed, Lollie Mercer and Dal flirting, Anne hysterical, and Jim making his will in the den! You will have to take Aunt Selina tonight, Kit; I'm all in."

"If you'll put her to bed, I'll keep her there," I conceded, after some parley.

"You're a dear." Bella came back from the door. "Look here, Kit, you know Jim pretty well. Don't you think he looks ill? Thinner?"

"He's a wreck," I said soberly. "You have a lot to answer for, Bella."

Bella went over to the cheval glass and looked in it. "I avoid him all I can," she said, posing. "He's awfully funny; he's so afraid I'll think he's serious about you. He can't realize that for me he simply doesn't exist."

Well, I took Aunt Selina, and about two o'clock, while I was in my first sleep, I woke to find her standing beside me, tugging at my arm.

"There's somebody in the house," she whispered. "Thieves!"

"If they're in they'll not get out tonight," I said.

"I tell you, I saw a man skulking on the stairs," she insisted.

I got up ungraciously enough, and put on my dressing gown. Aunt Selina, who had her hair in crimps, tied a veil over her head, and together we went to the head of the stairs. Aunt Selina leaned far over and peered down.

"He's in the library," she whispered. "I can see a light."

The lust of battle was in Aunt Selina's eye. She girded her robe about her and began to descend the stairs cautiously. We went through the hall and stopped at the library door. It was empty, but from the den beyond came a hum of voices and the cheerful glow of fire light. I realized the situation then, but it was too late.

"Then why did you kiss her in the dining room?" Bella was saying in her clear, high tones. "You did, didn't you?"

"It was only her hand," Jim, desperately explaining. "I've got to pay her some attention, under the circumstances. And I give you my word, I was thinking of you when I did it." *The wretch!*

Aunt Selina drew her breath in suddenly.

"I am thinking of marrying Reggie Wolfe." This was Bella, of course. "He wants me to. He's a dear boy."

"If you do, I will kill him."

"I am so very lonely," Bella sighed. We could hear the creak of Jim's shirt bosom that showed that he had sighed also. Aunt Selina had gripped me by the arm, and I could hear her breathing hard beside me.

"It's only Jim," I whispered. "I — I don't want to hear anymore."

But she clutched me firmly, and the next thing we heard was another creak, louder and —

"Get up! Get up off your knees this instant!" Bella was saying frantically. "Some one might come in."

"Don't send me away," Jim said in a smothered voice. "Everyone in the house is asleep, and I love you, dear."

Aunt Selina swallowed hard in the darkness.

"You have no right to make love to me," Bella. "It's — it's highly improper, under the circumstances."

And then Jim: "You swallow a camel and stick at a gnat. Why did you meet me here, if you didn't expect me to make love to you? I've stood for a lot, Bella, but this foolishness will have to end. Either you love me — or you don't. I'm desperate." He drew a long, forlorn breath.

"Poor old Jim!" This was Bella. A pause. Then — "Let my hand alone!" Also Bella.

"It is *my* hand!" — Jim's most fatuous tone. "*There* is where you wore my ring. There's the mark still." Sounds of Jim kissing Bella's ring finger. "What did you do with it? Throw it away?" More sounds.

Aunt Selina crossed the library swiftly, and again I followed. Bella was sitting in a low chair by the fire, looking at the logs, in the most exquisite negligee of pink chiffon and ribbon. Jim was on his knees, staring at her adoringly, and holding both her hands.

"I'll tell you a secret," Bella was saying, looking as coy as she knew how — which was considerable. "I — I still wear it, on a chain around my neck."

On a chain around her neck! Bella, who is décolleté whenever it is allowable, and more than is proper!

That was the limit of Aunt Selina's endurance. Still holding me, she stepped through the doorway and into the firelight, a fearful figure.

Jim saw her first. He went quite white and struggled to get

up, smiling a sickly smile. Bella, after her first surprise, was superbly indifferent. She glanced at us, raised her eyebrows, and then looked at the clock.

"More victims of insomnia!" she said. "Won't you come in? Jim, pull up a chair by the fire for your aunt."

Aunt Selina opened her mouth twice, like a fish, before she could speak. Then —

"James, I demand that that woman leave the house!" she said hoarsely.

Bella leaned back and yawned.

"James, shall I go?" she asked amiably.

"Nonsense," Jim said, pulling himself together as best he could. "Look here, Aunt Selina, you know she can't go out, and what's more, I — don't want her to go."

"You — what?" Aunt Selina screeched, taking a step forward. "You have the audacity to say such a thing to me!"

Bella leaned over and gave the fire log a punch.

"I was just saying that he shouldn't say such things to me, either," she remarked pleasantly. "I'm afraid you'll take cold, Miss Caruthers. Wouldn't you like a hot sherry flip?"

Aunt Selina gasped. Then she sat down heavily on one of the carved teakwood chairs.

"He said he loved you; I heard him," she said weakly. "He — he was going to put his arm around you!"

"Habit!" Jim put in, trying to smile. "You see, Aunt Selina, it's — well, it's a habit I got into some time ago, and I — my arm does it without my thinking about it."

"Habit!" Aunt Selina repeated, her voice thick with passion. Then she turned to me. "Go to your room at once!" she said in her most awful tone. "Go to your room and leave this — this shocking affair to me."

But if she had reached her limit, so had I. If Jim chose to ruin himself, it was not my fault. Anyone with common sense would have known at least to close the door before he went down on his knees, no matter to whom. So when Aunt Selina turned on me and pointed in the direction of the staircase, I did not move.

"I am perfectly wide awake," I said coldly. "I shall go to bed when I am entirely ready, and not before. And as for Jim's conduct, I do not know much about the conventions in such cases, but if he wishes to embrace Miss Knowles, and she wants him to, the situation is interesting, but hardly novel."

Aunt Selina rose slowly and drew the folds of her dressing gown around her, away from the contamination of my touch.

"Do you know what you are saying?" she demanded hoarsely.

"I do." I was quite white and stiff from my knees up, but below I was wavery. I glanced at Jim for moral support, but he was looking idolatrously at Bella. As for her, quite suddenly she had dropped her mask of indifference; her face was strained and anxious, and there were deep circles I had not seen before, under her eyes. And it was Bella who finally threw herself into the breach — the family breach.

"It is all my fault, Miss Caruthers," she said, stepping between Aunt Selina and myself. "I have been a blind and wicked woman, and I have almost wrecked two lives."

Two! What of mine?

"You see," she struggled on, against the glint in Aunt Selina's eyes. "I — I did not realize how much I cared, until it was too late. I did so many things that were cruel and wrong — oh, Jim, Jim!"

She turned and buried her head on his shoulder and cried; real tears. I could hardly believe that it was Bella. And Jim put both his arms around her and almost cried, too, and looked nauseatingly happy with the eye he turned to Bella, and scared to death out of the one he kept on Aunt Selina.

She turned on me, as of course I knew she would.

"That," she said, pointing at Jim and Bella, "that shameful picture is due to your own indifference. I am not blind; I have seen how you rejected all his loving advances." Bella drew away from Jim, but he jerked her back. "If anything in the world would reconcile me to divorce, it is this unbelievable situation. James, are you shameless?"

But James was and didn't care who knew it. And as there was nothing else to do, and no one else to do it, I stood very straight against the door frame, and told the whole miserable story from the very beginning. I told how Dal and Jim had persuaded me, and how I had weakened and found it was too late, and how Bella had come in that night, when she had no business to come, and had sat down in the basement kitchen on my hands and almost turned me into a raving maniac. As I went on I became fluent; my sense of injury grew on me. I made it perfectly clear that I hated them all, and that when people got divorces they ought to know their own minds and stay divorced. And at that a great light broke on Aunt Selina, who hadn't understood until that minute.

In view of her principles, she might have been expected to turn on Jim and Bella, and disinherit them, and cast them out, figuratively, with the flaming sword of her tongue. *But she did not!*

She turned on me in the most terrible way, and asked me how I dared to come between husband and wife, because divorce or no divorce, whom God hath joined together, and so on. And when Jim picked up his courage in both hands and tried to interfere, she pushed him back with one hand while she pointed the other at me and called me a Jezebel.

Chapter XIX
THE HARBISON MAN

She talked for an hour, having got between me and the door, and she scolded Jim and Bella thoroughly. But they did not hear it, being occupied with each other, sitting side by side meekly on the divan with Jim holding Bella's hand under a cushion. She said they would have to be very good to make up for all the deception, but it was perfectly clear that it was a relief to her to find that I didn't belong to her permanently, and as I have said before, she was crazy about Bella.

I sat back in a chair and grew comfortably drowsy in the monotony of her voice. It was a name that brought me to myself with a jerk.

"Mr. Harbison!" Aunt Selina was saying. "Then bring him down at once, James. I want no more deception. There is no use cleaning a house and leaving a dirty corner."

"It will not be necessary for me to stay and see it swept," I said, mustering the rags she had left of my self-respect, and trying to pass her. But she planted herself squarely before me.

"You can not stir up a dust like this, young woman, and leave other people to sneeze in it," she said grimly. And I stayed.

I sat, very small, on a chair in a corner. I felt like Jezebel, or whatever her name was, and now the Harbison man was coming, and he was going to see me stripped of my pretensions to domesticity and of a husband who neglected me. He was going to see me branded a living lie, and he would hate me because I had put him in a ridiculous position. He was just the sort to resent being ridiculous.

Jim brought him down in a dressing gown and a state of bewilderment. It was plain that the memory of the afternoon still rankled, for he was very short with Jim and inclined to resent the whole thing. The clock in the hall chimed half after three as they came down the stairs, and I heard Mr. Harbison stumble over something in the darkness and say that if it was a joke, he wasn't in the humor for it. To which Jim retorted that it wasn't anything resembling a joke, and for heaven's sake not to walk on his feet; he couldn't get around the furniture any faster.

At the door of the den Mr. Harbison stopped, blinking in the light. Then, when he saw us, he tried to back himself and his dishabille out into the obscurity of the library. But Aunt Selina was too quick for him.

"Come in," she called, "I want you, young man. It seems that there are only two fools in the house, and you are one."

He straightened at that and looked bewildered, but he tried to smile.

"I thought I was the only one," he said. "Is it possible that there is another?"

"I am the other," she announced. I think she expected him to say "Impossible," but, whatever he was, he was never banal.

"Is that so?" he asked politely, trying to be interested and to understand at the same time. He had not seen me. He was gazing fixedly at Bella, languishing on the divan and watching him with lowered lids, and he had given Jim a side glance of contempt. But now he saw me and he colored under his tan. His neck blushed furiously, being much whiter than his face. He kept his eyes on mine, and I knew that he was mutely asking forgiveness. But the thought of what was coming paralyzed me. My eyes were glued to his as they had been that first evening when he had called me "Mrs. Wilson," and after an instant he looked away, and his face was set and hard.

"It seems that we have all been playing a little comedy, Mr. Harbison," Aunt Selina began, nasally sarcastic. "Or rather, you and I have been the audience. The rest have played."

"I — I don't think I understand," he said slowly. "I have seen very little comedy."

"It was not well planned," Aunt Selina retorted tartly. "The idea was good, but the young person who was playing the part of Mrs. Wilson — overacted."

"Oh, come, Aunt Selina," Jim protested, "Kit was coaxed and cajoled into this thing. Give me fits if you like; I deserve all I get. But let Kit alone — she did it for me."

Bella looked over at me and smiled nastily.

"I would stop doing things for Jim, Kit," she said. "It is *so* unprofitable."

But Mr. Harbison harked back to Aunt Selina's speech.

"*Playing* the part of Mrs. Wilson!" he repeated. "Do you mean — ?

"Exactly. Playing the part. She is not Mrs. Wilson. It seems that that honor belonged at one time to Miss Knowles. I believe such things are not unknown in New York, only why in the name of sense does a man want to divorce a woman and then meet her at two o'clock in the morning to kiss the place where his own wedding ring used to rest?"

Jim fidgeted. Bella was having spasms of mirth to herself, but the Harbison man did not smile. He stood for a moment looking at the fire; then he thrust his hands deep into the pockets of his dressing gown, and stalked over to me. He did not care that the others were watching and listening.

"Is it true?" he demanded, staring down at me. "You are *not* Mrs. Wilson? You are not married at all? All that about being neglected — and loathing *him*, and all that on the roof — there was no foundation of truth?"

I could only shake my head without looking up. There was no defense to be made. Oh, I deserved the scorn in his voice.

"They — they persuaded you, I suppose, and it was to help somebody? It was not a practical joke?"

"No," I rallied a little spirit at that. It had been anything but a joke.

He drew a long breath.

"I think I understand," he said slowly, "but — you could have saved me something. I must have given you all a great deal of amusement."

"Oh, no," I protested. "I — I want to tell you —"

But he deliberately left me and went over to the door. There he turned and looked down at Aunt Selina. He was a little white, but there was no passion in his face.

"Thank you for telling me all this, Miss Caruthers," he said easily. "Now that you and I know, I'm afraid the others will miss their little diversion. Good night."

Oh, it was all right for Jim to laugh and say that he was only huffed a little and would be over it by morning. I knew better. There was something queer in his face as he went out. He did not even glance in my direction. He had said very little, but he had put me as effectually in the wrong as if he had not kissed me — deliberately kissed me — that very evening, on the roof.

I did not go to sleep again. I lay wretchedly thinking things over and trying to remember who Jezebel was, and toward morning I distinctly heard the knob of the door turn. I mistrusted my ears, however, and so I got up quietly and went over in the darkness. There was no sound outside, but when I put my hand on the knob I felt it move under my fingers. The counter pressure evidently alarmed whoever it was, for the knob was released and nothing more happened. But by this time anything so uncomplicated as the fumbling of a knob at night had no power to disturb me. I went back to bed.

Chapter XX
BREAKING OUT IN A NEW PLACE

*H*unger roused everybody early the next morning, Friday. Leila Mercer had discovered a box of bonbons that she had forgotten, and we divided them around. Aunt Selina asked for the candied fruit and got it — quite a third of the box. We gathered in the lower hall and on the stairs and nibbled nauseating sweets while Mr. Harbison examined the telephone.

He did not glance in my direction. Betty and Dal were helping him, and he seemed very cheerful. Max sat with me on the stairs. Mr. Harbison had just unscrewed the telephone box from the wall and was squinting into it, when Bella came downstairs. It was her first appearance, but as she was always late, nobody noticed. When she stopped, just above us on the stairs, however, we looked up, and she was holding to the rail and trembling perceptibly.

"Mr. Harbison, will you — can you come upstairs?" she asked. Her voice was strained, almost reedy, and her lips were white.

Mr. Harbison stared up at her, with the telephone box in his hands.

"Why — er — certainly," he said, "but, unless it's very important, I'd like to fix this talking machine. We want to make a food record."

"I'd like to break a food record," Max put in, but Bella

created a diversion by sitting down suddenly on the stair just above us, and burying her face in her handkerchief.

"Jim is sick," she said, with a sob. "He — he doesn't want anything to eat, and his head aches. He — said for me — to go away and let him die!"

Dal dropped the hammer immediately, and Lollie Mercer sat petrified, with a bonbon halfway to her mouth. For, of course, it was unexpected, finding sentiment of any kind in Bella, and none of them knew about the scene in the den in the small hours of the morning.

"Sick!" Aunt Selina said, from a hall chair. "Sick! Where?"

"All over," Bella quavered. "His poor head is hot, and he's thirsty, but he doesn't want anything but water."

"Great Scott!" Dal said suddenly. "Suppose he should — Bella, are you telling us *all* his symptoms?"

Bella put down her handkerchief and got up. From her position on the stairs she looked down on us with something of her old haughty manner.

"If he is ill, you may blame yourselves, all of you," she said cruelly. "You taunted him with being — fat, and laughed at him, until he stopped eating the things he should eat. And he has been exercising — on the roof, until he has worn himself out. And now — he is ill. He — he has a rash."

Everybody jumped at that, and we instinctively moved away from Bella. She was quite cold and scornful by that time.

"A rash!" Max exclaimed. "What sort of rash?"

"I did not see it," Bella said with dignity, and turning, she went up the stairs.

There was a great deal of excitement, and nobody except Mr. Harbison was willing to go near Jim. He went up at once with Bella, while Max and Dal sat cravenly downstairs and wondered if we would all take it, and Anne told about a man she knew who had it, and was deaf and dumb and blind when he recovered.

Mr. Harbison came down after a while, and said that the rash was there, right enough, and that Jim absolutely refused to be quarantined; that he insisted that he always got a rash from early strawberries and that if he *did* have anything, since they were so touchy he hoped they would all get it. If they locked him in he would kick the door down.

We had a long conference in the hall, with Bella sitting red-eyed and objecting to every suggestion we made. And finally we arranged to shut Jim up in one of the servants' bedrooms with a sheet wrung out of disinfectant hung over the door. Bella said she would sit outside in the hall and read to him through the closed door, so finally he gave a grudging consent. But he was in an awful humor. Max and Dal put on rubber gloves and helped him over, and they said afterward that the way he talked was fearful. And there was a telephone in the maid's room, and he kept asking for things every five minutes.

When the doctor came he said it was too early to tell positively, and he ordered him liquid diet and said he would be back that evening.

Which — the diet — takes me back to the famine. After they had moved Jim, Mr. Harbison went back to the telephone, and found everything as it should be. So he followed the telephone wire, and the rest followed him. I did not; he had systematically ignored me all morning, after having dared to kiss me the night before. And any other man I know, after looking at me the way he had looked a dozen times, would have been at least reasonably glad to find me free and unmarried. But it was clear that he was not; I wondered if he was the kind of man who always makes love to the other man's wife and runs like mad when she is left a widow, or gets a divorce.

And just when I had decided that I hated him, and that there was one man I knew who would never make love to a woman whom he thought married and then be very dignified and aloof when he found she wasn't, I heard what was wrong with the telephone wire.

It had been cut! Cut through with a pair of silver manicure scissors from the dressing table in Bella's room, where Aunt Selina slept! The wire had been clipped where it came into the house, just under a window, and the scissors still lay on the sill.

It was mysterious enough, but no one was interested in the mystery just then. We wanted food, and wanted it at once. Mr. Harbison fixed the wire, and the first thing we did, of course, was to order something to eat. Aunt Selina went to bed just after luncheon with indigestion, to the relief of everyone in the house. She had been most unpleasant all morning.

When she found herself ill, however, she insisted on having Bella, and that made trouble at once. We found Bella with her cheek against the door into Jim's room, looking maudlin while he shouted love messages to her from the other side. At first she refused to stir, but after Anne and Max had tried and failed, the rest of us went to her in a body and implored her. We said Aunt Selina was in awful shape — which she was, as to temper — and that she had thrown a mustard plaster at Anne, which was true.

So Bella went, grumbling, and Jim was a maniac. We had not thought it would be so bad for Bella, but Aunt Selina fell asleep soon after she took charge, holding Bella's hand, and slept for three hours and never let go!

About two that afternoon the sun came out, and the rest of us went to the roof. The sleet had melted and the air was fairly warm. Two housemaids dusting rugs on the top of the next house came over and stared at us, and somebody in an automobile down on Riverside Drive stood up and waved at us. It was very cheerful and hopelessly lonely.

I stayed on the roof after the others had gone, and for some time I thought I was alone. After a while, I got a whiff of smoke, and then I saw Mr. Harbison far over in the corner, one foot on the parapet, moodily smoking a pipe. He was gazing out over the river, and paying no attention to me. This was natural, considering that I had hardly spoken to him all day.

I would not let him drive me away, so I sat still, and it grew darker and colder. He filled his pipe now and then, but he never looked in my direction. Finally, however, as it grew very dusk, he knocked the ashes out and came toward me.

"I am going to make a request, Miss McNair," he said evenly. "Please keep off the roof after sunset. There are — reasons." I had risen and was preparing to go downstairs.

"Unless I know the reasons, I refuse to do anything of the kind," I retorted. He bowed.

"Then the door will be kept locked," he rejoined, and opened it for me. He did not follow me, but stood watching until I was down, and I heard him close the roof door firmly behind me.

Chapter XXI
A BAR OF SOAP

*L*ate that evening Betty Mercer and Dallas were writing verses of condolence to be signed by all of us and put under the door into Jim's room when Bella came running down the stairs.

Dal was reading the first verse when she came. "Listen to this, Bella," he said triumphantly:

"There was a fat artist named Jas,
   Who cruelly called his friends nas.
   When, altho' shut up tight,
   He broke out over night
   With a rash that is maddening, he clas."

Then he caught sight of Bella's face as she stood in the doorway, and stopped.

"Jim is delirious!" she announced tragically. "You shut him in there all alone and now he's delirious. I'll never forgive any of you."

"Delirious!" everybody exclaimed.

"He was sane enough when I took him his chicken broth," Mr. Harbison said. "He was almost fluent."

"He is stark, staring crazy," Bella insisted hysterically. "I — I locked the door carefully when I went down to my dinner, and when I came up it — it was unlocked, and Jim was babbling on the bed, with a sheet over his face. He — he says the house is haunted and he wants all the men to come up and sit in the room with him."

"Not on your life," Max said. "I am young, and my career has only begun. I don't intend to be cut off in the flower of my youth. But I'll tell you what I will do; I'll take him a drink. I can tie it to a pole or something."

But Mr. Harbison did not smile. He was thoughtful for a minute. Then:

"I don't believe he is delirious," he said quietly, "and I wouldn't be surprised if he has happened on something that — will be of general interest. I think I will stay with him tonight."

After that, of course, none of the others would confess that he was afraid, so with the South American leading, they all went upstairs. The women of the party sat on the lower steps and listened, but everything was quiet. Now and then we could hear the sound of voices, and after a while there was a rapid slamming of doors and the sound of some one running down to the second floor. Then quiet again.

None of us felt talkative. Bella had followed the men up and had been put out, and sat sniffling by herself in the den. Aunt Selina was working over a jig-saw puzzle in the library, and declaring that some of it must be lost. Anne and Leila Mercer were embroidering, and Betty and I sat idle, our hands in our laps. The whole atmosphere of the house was mysterious. Anne told over again of the strange noises the night her necklace was stolen. Betty asked me about the time when the comfort slipped from under my fingers. And when, in the midst of the story, the telephone rang, we all jumped and shrieked.

In an hour or so they sent for Flannigan, and he went upstairs. He came down again soon, however, and returned with something over his arm that looked like a rope. It seemed to be made of all kinds of things tied together, trunk straps, clothesline, bed sheets, and something that Flannigan pointed to with rage and said he hadn't been able to keep his clothes on all day. He refused to explain further, however, and trailed the nondescript article up the stairs. We could only gaze after him and wonder what it all meant.

The conclave lasted far into the night. The feminine contingent went to bed, but not to sleep. Some time after midnight, Mr. Harbison and Max went downstairs and I could hear them rattling around testing windows and burglar alarms. But finally everyone settled down and the rest of the night was quiet.

Betty Mercer came into my room the next morning, Sunday, and said Anne Brown wanted me. I went over at once, and Anne was sitting up in bed, crying. Dal had slipped out of the room at daylight, she said, and hadn't come back. He had thought she was asleep, but she wasn't, and she knew he was dead, for nothing ever made Dal get up on Sunday before noon.

There was no one moving in the house, and I hardly knew what to do. It was Betty who said she would go up and rouse Mr. Harbison and Max, who had taken Jim's place in the studio. She started out bravely enough, but in a minute we heard her flying back. Anne grew perfectly white.

"He's lying on the upper stairs!" Betty cried, and we all ran out. It was quite true. Dal was lying on the stairs in a bathrobe, with one of Jim's Indian war clubs in his hand. And he was sound asleep.

He looked somewhat embarrassed when he roused and saw us standing around. He said he was going to play a practical joke on somebody and fell asleep in the middle of it. And Anne said he wasn't even an intelligent liar, and went back to bed in a temper. But Betty came in with me, and we sat and looked at each other and didn't say much. The situation was beyond us.

The doctor let Jim out the next day, there having been nothing the matter with him but a stomach rash. But Jim was changed; he mooned around Bella, of course, as before, but he was abstracted at times, and all that day — Sunday — he wandered off by himself, and one would come across him unexpectedly in the basement or along some of the unused back halls.

Aunt Selina held service that morning. Jim said that he always had a prayer book, but that he couldn't find anything with so many people in the house. So Aunt Selina read some religious poetry out of the newspapers, and gave us a valuable talk on Deception versus Honesty, with me as the illustration.

Almost everybody took a nap after luncheon. I stayed in

the den and read Ibsen, and felt very mournful. And after
Hedda had shot herself, I lay down on the divan and cried a
little — over Hedda; she was young and it was such a tragic
ending — and then I fell asleep.

When I wakened Mr. Harbison was standing by the table,
and he held my book in his hands. In view of the armed
neutrality between us, I expected to see him bow to me curtly,
turn on his heel and leave the room. Indeed, considering his
state of mind the night before, I should hardly have been
surprised if he had thrown Hedda at my head. (This is not a
pun. I detest them.) But instead, when he heard me move he
glanced over at me and even smiled a little.

"She wasn't worth it," he said, indicating the book.

"Worth what?"

"Your tears. You were crying over it, weren't you?"

"She was very unhappy," I asserted indifferently. "She was
married and she loved some one else."

"Do you really think she did?" he asked. "And even so, was
that a reason?"

"The other man cared for her; he may not have been able
to help it."

"But he knew that she was married," he said virtuously,
and then he caught my eye and he saw the analogy instantly,
for he colored hotly and put down the book.

"Most men argue that way," I said. "They argue by the
book, and — they do as they like."

He picked up a Japanese ivory paper weight from the table,
and stood balancing it across his finger.

"You are perfectly right," he said at last. "I deserve it all.
My grievance is at myself. Your — your beauty, and the fact
that I thought you were unhappy, put me — beside myself. It
is not an excuse; it is a weak explanation. I will not forget
myself again."

He was as abject as anyone could have wished. It was my
minute of triumph, but I can not pretend that I was happy.
Evidently it had been only a passing impulse. If he had really
cared, now that he knew I was free, he would have forgotten
himself again at once. Then a new explanation occurred to
me. Suppose it had been Bella all the time, and the real shock
had been to find that she had been married!

"The fault of the situation was really mine," I said magnanimously; "I quite blame myself. Only, you must believe one thing. You never furnished us any amusement." I looked at him sidewise. "The discovery that Bella and Jim were once married must have been a great shock."

"It was a surprise," he replied evenly. His voice and his eyes were inscrutable. He returned my glance steadily. It was infuriating to have gone half-way to meet him, as I had, and then to find him entrenched in his self-sufficiency again. I got up.

"It is unfortunate that our acquaintance has begun so unfavorably," I remarked, preparing to pass him. "Under other circumstances we might have been friends."

"There is only one solace," he said. "When we do not have friends, we can not lose them."

He opened the door to let me pass out, and as our eyes met, all the coldness died out of his. He held out his hand, but I was hurt. I refused to see it.

"Kit!" he said unsteadily. "I — I'm an obstinate, pig-headed brute. I am sorry. Can't we be friends, after all?"

"'When we do not have friends we can not lose them,'" I replied with cool malice. And the next instant the door closed behind me.

It was that night that the really serious event of the quarantine occurred.

We were gathered in the library, and everybody was deadly dull. Aunt Selina said she had been reared to a strict observance of the Sabbath, and she refused to go to bed early. The cards and card tables were put away and everyone sat around and quarreled and was generally nasty, except Bella and Jim, who had gone into the den just after dinner and firmly closed the door.

I think it was just after Max proposed to me. Yes, he proposed to me again that night. He said that Jim's illness had decided him; that any of us might take sick and die, shut in that contaminated atmosphere, and that if he did he wanted it all settled. And whether I took him or not he wanted me to remember him kindly if anything happened. I really hated to refuse him — he was in such deadly earnest. But it was quite unnecessary for him to have blamed his refusal, as

he did, on Mr. Harbison. I am sure I had refused him plenty
of times before I had ever heard of the man. Yes, it was just
after he proposed to me that Flannigan came to the door and
called Mr. Harbison out into the hall.

Flannigan — like most of the people in the house — always
went to Mr. Harbison when there was anything to be done.
He openly adored him, and — what was more — he did what
Mr. Harbison ordered without a word, while the rest of us
had to get down on our knees and beg.

Mr. Harbison went out, muttering something about a
storm coming up, and seeing that the tent was secure. Betty
Mercer went with him. She had been at his heels all evening,
and called him "Tom" on every possible occasion. Indeed, she
made no secret of it; she said that she was mad about him,
and that she would love to live in South America, and have
an Indian squaw for a lady's maid, and sit out on the veranda
in the evenings and watch the Southern Cross shooting across
the sky, and eat tropical food from the quaint Indian pottery.
She was not even daunted when Dal told her the Southern
Cross did not shoot, and that the food was probably canned
corn on tin dishes.

So Betty went with him. She wore a pale yellow dinner
gown, with just a sophisticated touch of black here and there,
and cut modestly square in the neck. Her shoulders are
scrawny. And after they were gone — not her shoulders; Mr.
Harbison and she — Aunt Selina announced that the next
day was Monday, that she had only a week's supply of
clothing with her, and that no policeman who ever swung a
mace should wash her undergarments for her.

She paused a moment, but nobody offered to do it. Anne
was reading De Maupassant under cover of a table, and the
rest pretended not to hear. After a pause, Aunt Selina got up
heavily and went upstairs, coming down soon after with a
bundle covered with a green shawl, and with a white balbrig-
gan stocking trailing from an opening in it. She paused at
the library door, surveyed the inmates, caught my unlucky
eye and beckoned to me with a relentless forefinger.

"We can put them to soak tonight," she confided to me,
"and tomorrow they will be quite simple to do. There is no
lace to speak of" — Dal raised his eyebrows — "and very little

flouncing."

Aunt Selina and I went to the laundry. It never occurred to anyone that Bella should have gone; she had stepped into all my privileges — such as they were — and assumed none of my obligations. Aunt Selina and I went to the laundry.

It is strange what big things develop from little ones. In this case it was a bar of soap. And if Flannigan had used as much soap as he should have instead of washing up the kitchen floor with cold dish water, it would have developed sooner. The two most unexpected events of the whole quarantine occurred that night at the same time, one on the roof and one in the cellar. The cellar one, although curious, was not so serious as the other, so it comes first.

Aunt Selina put her clothes in a tub in the laundry and proceeded to dress them like a vegetable. She threw in a handful of salt, some kerosene oil and a little ammonia. The result was villainous, but after she tasted it — or snuffed it — she said it needed a bar of soap cut up to give it strength — or flavor — and I went into the store room for it.

The laundry soap was in a box. I took in a silver fork, for I hated to touch the stuff, and jabbed a bar successfully in the semi-darkness. Then I carried it back to the laundry and dropped it on the table. Aunt Selina looked at the fork with disgust; then we both looked at the soap. *One side of it was covered with round holes that curved around on each other like a coiled snake.*

I ran back to the store room, and there, a little bit sticky and smelling terribly of rosin, lay Anne's pearl necklace!

I was so excited that I seized Aunt Selina by the hands and danced her all over the place. Then I left her, trying to find her hair pins on the floor, and ran up to tell the others. I met Betty in the hall and waved the pearls at her. But she did not notice them.

"Is Mr. Harbison down there?" she asked breathlessly. "I left him on the roof and went down to my room for my scarf, and when I went back he had disappeared. He — he doesn't seem to be in the house." She tried to laugh, but her voice was shaky. "He couldn't have got down without passing me, anyhow," she supplemented. "I suppose I'm silly, but so many queer things have happened, Kit."

"I wouldn't worry, Betty," I soothed her. "He is big enough to take care of himself. And with the best intentions in the world, you can't have him all the time, you know."

She was too much startled to be indignant. She followed me into the library, where the sight of the pearls produced a tremendous excitement, and then everyone had to go down to the store room, and see where the necklace had been hidden, and Max examined all the bars of soap for thumb prints.

Mr. Harbison did not appear. Max commented on the fact caustically, but Dal hushed him up. And so, Anne hugging her pearls, and Aunt Selina having put a final seasoning of washing powder on the clothes in the tub, we all went upstairs to bed. It had been a long day, and the morning would at least bring bridge.

I was almost ready for bed when Jim tapped at my door. I had been very cool to him since the night in the library when I was publicly staked and martyred, and he was almost cringing when I opened the door.

"What is it now?" I asked cruelly. "Has Bella tired of it already, or has somebody else a rash?"

"Don't be a shrew, Kit," he said. "I don't want you to do anything. I only — when did you see Harbison last?"

"If you mean 'last,'" I retorted, "I'm afraid I haven't seen the last of him yet." Then I saw that he was really worried. "Betty was leading him to the roof," I added. "Why? Is he missing?"

"He isn't anywhere in the house. Dal and I have been over every inch of it." Max had come up, in a dressing gown, and was watching me insolently.

"I think we have seen the last of him," he said. "I'm sorry, Kit, to nip the little romance in the bud. The fellow was crazy about you — there's no doubt of it. But I've been watching him from the beginning, and I think I'm upheld. Whether he went down the water spout, or across a board to the next house —"

"I — I dislike him intensely," I said angrily, "but you would not dare to say that to his face. He could strangle you with one hand."

Max laughed disagreeably.

"Well, I only hope he is gone," he threw at me over his shoulder, "I wouldn't want to be responsible to your father if he had stayed." I was speechless with wrath.

They went away then, and I could hear them going over the house. At one o'clock Jim went up to bed, the last, and Mr. Harbison had not been found. I did not see how they could go to bed at all. If he had escaped, then Max was right and the whole thing was heart-breaking. And if he had not, then he might be lying —

I got up and dressed.

The early part of the night had been cloudy, but when I got to the roof it was clear starlight. The wind blew through the electric wires strung across and set them singing. The occasional bleat of a belated automobile on the drive below came up to me raucously. The tent gleamed, a starlit ghost of itself, and the boxwoods bent in the breeze. I went over to the parapet and leaned my elbows on it. I had done the same thing so often before; I had carried all my times of stress so infallibly to that particular place, that instinctively my feet turned there.

And there in the starlight, I went over the whole serio-comedy, and I loathed my part in it. He had been perfectly right to be angry with me and with all of us. And I had been a hypocrite and a Pharisee, and had thanked God that I was not as other people, when the fact was that I was worse than the worst. And although it wasn't dignified to think of him going down the drain pipe, still — no one could blame him for wanting to get away from us, and he was quite muscular enough to do it.

I was in the depths of self-abasement when I heard a sound behind me. It was a long breath, quite audible, that ended in a groan. I gripped the parapet and listened, while my heart pounded, and in a minute it came again.

I was terribly frightened. Then — I don't know how I did it, but I was across the roof, kneeling beside the tent, where it stood against the chimney. And there, lying prone among the flower pots, and almost entirely hidden, lay the man we had been looking for.

His head was toward me, and I reached out shakingly and touched his face. It was cold, and my hand, when I drew it back, was covered with blood.

Chapter XXII
IT WAS DELIRIUM

I was sure he was dead. He did not move, and when I caught his hands and called him frantically, he did not hear me. And so, with the horror over me, I half fell down the stairs and roused Jim in the studio.

They all came with lights and blankets, and they carried him into the tent and put him on the couch and tried to put whisky in his mouth. But he could not swallow. And the silence became more and more ominous until finally Anne got hysterical and cried, "He is dead! Dead!" and collapsed on the roof.

But he was not. Just as the lights in the tent began to have red rings around them and Jim's voice came from away across the river, somebody said, "There, he swallowed that," and soon after, he opened his eyes. He muttered something that sounded like "Andean pinnacle" and lapsed into unconsciousness again. But he was not dead! He was not dead!

When the doctor came they made a stretcher out of one of Jim's six-foot canvases — it had a picture on it, and Jim was angry enough the next day — and took him down to the studio. We made it as much like a sick-room as we could, and we tried to make him comfortable. But he lay without opening his eyes, and at dawn the doctor brought a consultant and a trained nurse.

The nurse was an offensively capable person. She put us all out, and scolded Anne for lighting Japanese incense in the room — although Anne explained that it is very reviving. And she said that it was unnecessary to have a dozen people breathing up all the oxygen and asphyxiating the patient. She was good-looking, too. I disliked her at once. Anyone could see by the way she took his pulse — just letting his poor hand hang, without any support — that she was a purely mechanical creature, without heart.

Well, as I said before, she put us all out, and shut the door, and asked us not to whisper outside. Then, too, she refused to allow any flowers in the room, although Betty had got a florist out of bed to order some.

The consultant came, stayed an hour, and left. Aunt Selina, who proved herself a trump in that trying time, waylaid him in the hall, and he said it might be a fractured skull, although it was possibly only concussion.

The men spent most of the morning together in the den, with the door shut. Now and then one of them would tiptoe upstairs, ask the nurse how her patient was doing, and creak down again. Just before noon they all went to the roof and examined again the place where he had been found. I know, for I was in the upper hall outside the studio. I stayed there almost all day, and after a while the nurse let me bring her things as she needed them. I don't know why mother didn't let me study nursing — I always wanted to do it. And I felt helpless and childish now, when there were things to be done.

Max came down from the roof alone, and I cornered him in the upper hall.

"I'm going crazy, Max," I said. "Nobody will tell me anything, and I can't stand it. How was he hurt? Who hurt him?"

Max looked at me quite a long time.

"I'm darned if I understand you, Kit," he said gravely. "You said you disliked Harbison."

"So I do — I did," I supplemented. "But whether I like him or not has nothing to do with it. He has been injured — perhaps murdered" — I choked a little. "Which — which of you did it?"

Max took my hand and held it, looking down at me.

"I wish you could have cared for me like that," he said gently. "Dear little girl, we don't know who hurt him. I didn't, if that's what you mean. Perhaps a flower pot —"

I began to cry then, and he drew me to him and let me cry on his arm. He stood very quietly, patting my head in a brotherly way and behaving very well, save that once he said:

"Don't cry too long, Kit; I can stand only a certain amount."

And just then the nurse opened the door to the studio, and with Max's arm still around me, I raised my head and looked in.

Mr. Harbison was conscious. His eyes were open, and he was staring at us both as we stood framed by the doorway.

He lay back at once and closed his eyes, and the nurse shut the door. There was no use, even if I had been allowed in, in trying to explain to him. To attempt such a thing would have been to presume that he was interested in an explanation. I thought bitterly to myself as I brought the nurse cracked ice and struggled to make beef tea in the kitchen, that lives had been wrecked on less.

Dal was allowed ten minutes in the sick room during the afternoon, and he came out looking puzzled and excited. He refused to tell us what he had learned, however, and the rest of the afternoon he and Jim spent in the cellar.

The day dragged on. Downstairs people ate and read and wrote letters, and outside newspaper men talked together and gazed over at the house and photographed the doctors coming in and the doctors going out. As for me, in the intervals of bringing things, I sat in Bella's chair in the upper hall, and listened to the crackle of the nurse's starched skirts.

At midnight that night the doctors made a thorough examination. When they came out they were smiling.

"He is doing very well," the younger one said — he was hairy and dark, but he was beautiful to me. "He is entirely conscious now, and in about an hour you can send the nurse off for a little sleep. Don't let him talk."

And so at last I went through the familiar door into an unfamiliar room, with basins and towels and bottles around, and a screen made of Jim's largest canvases. And someone on the improvised bed turned and looked at me. He did not speak, and I sat down beside him. After a while he put his hand over mine as it lay on the bed.

"You are much better to me than I deserve," he said softly.

And because his eyes were disconcerting, I put an ice cloth over them.

"Much better than you deserve," I said, and patted the ice cloth to place gently. He fumbled around until he found my hand again, and we were quiet for a long time. I think he dozed, for he roused suddenly and pulled the cloth from his eyes.

"The — the day is all confused," he said, turning to look at me, "but — one thing seems to stand out from everything else. Perhaps it was delirium, but I seemed to see that door over there open, and you, outside, with — with Max. His arms were around you."

"It was delirium," I said softly. It was my final lie in that house of mendacity.

He drew a satisfied breath, and lifting my hand, held it to his lips and kissed it.

"I can hardly believe it is you," he said. "I have to hold firmly to your hand or you will disappear. Can't you move your chair closer? You are miles away." So I did it, for he was not to be excited.

After a little —

"It's awfully good of you to do this. I have been desperately sorry, Kit, about the other night. It was a ruffianly thing to do — to kiss you, when I thought —"

"You are to keep very still," I reminded him. He kissed my hand again, but he persisted.

"I was mad — crazy." I tried to give him some medicine, but he pushed the spoon aside. "You will have to listen," he said. "I am in the depths of self-disgust. I — I can't think of anything else. You see, you seemed so convinced that I was the blackguard that somehow nothing seemed to matter."

"I have forgotten it all," I declared generously, "and I would be quite willing to be friends, only, you remember you said —"

"Friends!" his voice was suddenly reckless, and he raised on his elbow. "Friends! Who wants to be friends? Kit, I was almost delirious that night. The instant I held you in my arms — It was all over. I loved you the first time I saw you. I — I suppose I'm a fool to talk like this."

And, of course, just then Dallas had to open the door and step into the room. He was covered with dirt and he had a hatchet in his hand.

"A rope!" he demanded, without paying any attention to us and diving into corners of the room. "Good heavens, isn't there a rope in this confounded house!"

He turned and rushed out, without any explanation, and left us staring at the door.

"Bother the rope!" I found myself forced to look into two earnest eyes. "Kit, were you *very* angry when I kissed you that night on the roof?"

"Very," I maintained stoutly.

"Then prepare yourself for another attack of rage!" he said. And Betty opened the door.

She had on a fetching pale blue dressing gown, and one braid of her yellow hair was pulled carelessly over her shoulder. When she saw me on my knees beside the bed (oh, yes, I forgot to say that, quite unconsciously, I had slid into that position) she stopped short, just inside the door, and put her hand to her throat. She stood for quite a perceptible time looking at us, and I tried to rise. But Tom shamelessly put his arm around my shoulders and held me beside him. Then Betty took a step back and steadied herself by the door frame. She had really cared, I knew then, but I was too excited to be sorry for her.

"I — I beg your pardon for coming in," she said nervously. "But — they want you downstairs, Kit. At least, I thought you would want to go, but — perhaps —"

Just then from the lower part of the house came a pandemonium of noises; women screaming, men shouting, and the sound of hatchet strokes and splintering wood. I seized Betty by the arm, and together we rushed down the stairs.

Chapter XXIII

COMING

*T*he second floor was empty. A table lay overturned at the top of the stairs, and a broken flower vase was weltering in its own ooze. Part way down Betty stepped on something sharp, that proved to be the Japanese paper knife from the den. I left her on the stairs examining her foot and hurried to the lower floor.

Here everything was in the utmost confusion. Aunt Selina had fainted, and was sitting in a hall chair with her head rolled over sidewise and the poker from the library fireplace across her knees. No one was paying any attention to her. And Jim was holding the front door open, while three of the guards hesitated in the vestibule. The noises continued from the back of the house, and as I stood on the lowest stair Bella came out from the dining room, with her face streaked with soot, and carrying a kettle of hot water.

"Jim," she called wildly. "While Max and Dal are below, you can pour this down from the top. It's boiling."

Jim glanced back over his shoulder. "Carry out your own murderous designs," he said. And then, as she started back with it, "Bella, for Heaven's sake," he called, "have you gone stark mad? Put that kettle down."

She did it sulkily and Jim turned to the policeman.

"Yes, I know it was a false alarm before," he explained patiently, "but this is genuine. It is just as I tell you. Yes, Flannigan is in the house somewhere, but he's hiding, I guess. We could manage the thing very well ourselves, but we have no cartridges for our revolvers." Then as the noise from the rear redoubled, "If you don't come in and help, I will telephone for the fire department," he concluded emphatically.

I ran to Aunt Selina and tried to straighten her head. In a moment she opened her eyes, sat up and stared around her. She saw the kettle at once.

"What are you doing with boiling water on the floor?" she said to me, with her returning voice. "Don't you know you will spoil the floor?" The ruling passion was strong with Aunt Selina, as usual.

I could not find out the trouble from anyone; people appeared and disappeared, carrying strange articles. Anne with a rope, Dal with his hatchet, Bella and the kettle, but I could get a coherent explanation from no one. When the guards finally decided that Jim was in earnest, and that the rest of us were not crawling out a rear window while he held them at the door, they came in, three of them and two reporters, and Jim led them to the butler's pantry.

Here we found Anne, very white and shaky, with the pantry table and two chairs piled against the door of the kitchen slide, and clutching the chamois-skin bag that held her jewels. She had a bottle of burgundy open beside her, and was pouring herself a glass with shaking hands when we appeared. She was furious at Jim.

"I very nearly fainted," she said hysterically. "I might have been murdered, and no one would have cared. I wish they would stop that chopping, I'm so nervous I could scream."

Jim took the Burgundy from her with one hand and pointed the police to the barricaded door with the other.

"That is the door to the dumb-waiter shaft," he said. "The lower one is fastened on the inside, in some manner. The noises commenced about eleven o'clock, while Mr. Brown was on guard. There were scraping sounds first, and later the sound of a falling body. He roused Mr. Reed and myself, but when we examined the shaft everything was quiet, and dark. We tried lowering a candle on a string, but — it was extinguished from below."

The reporters were busily removing the table and chairs from the door.

"If you have a rope handy," one of them said, "I will go

down the shaft."

(Dal says that all reporters should have been policemen, and that all policemen are natural newsgatherers.)

"The cage appears to be stuck, half-way between the floors," Jim said. "They are cutting through the door in the kitchen below."

They opened the door then and cautiously peered down, but there was nothing to be seen. I touched Jim gingerly on the arm.

"Is it — is it Flannigan,:" I asked, "shut in there?"

"No — yes — I don't know," he returned absently. "Run along and don't bother, Kit. He may take to shooting any minute."

Anne and I went out then and shut the door, and went into the dining room and sat on our feet, for of course the bullets might come up through the floor. Aunt Selina joined us there, and Bella, and the Mercer girls, and we sat around and talked in whispers, and Leila Mercer told of the time her grandfather had had a struggle with an escaped lunatic.

In the midst of the excitement Tom appeared in a bathrobe, looking very pale, with a bandage around his head, and the nurse at his heels threatening to leave and carrying a bottle of medicine and a spoon. He went immediately to the pantry, and soon we could hear him giving orders and the rest hurrying around to obey them. The hammering ceased, and the silence was even worse. It was more suggestive.

In about fifteen minutes there was a thud, as if the cage had fallen, and the sound of feet rushing down the cellar stairs. Then there were groans and loud oaths, and everybody talking at once, below, and the sound of a struggle. In the dining room we all sat bent forward, with straining ears and quickened breath, until we distinctly heard someone laugh. Then we knew that, whatever it was, it was over, and nobody was killed.

The sounds came closer, were coming up the stairs and into the pantry. Then the door swung open, and Tom and a policeman appeared in the doorway, with the others crowding behind. Between them they supported a grimy, unshaven object, covered with whitewash from the wall of the shaft, an object that had its hands fastened together with handcuffs, and that leered at us with a pair of the most villainously crossed eyes I have ever seen.

None of us had ever seen him before,

"Mr. Lawrence McGuirk, better known as Tubby,'" Tom said cheerfully. "A celebrity in his particular line, which is second-story man and all-round rascal. A victim of the quarantine, like ourselves."

"We've missed him for a week," one of the guards said with a grin. "We've been real anxious about you, Tubby. Ain't a week goes by, when you're in health, that we don't hear something of you."

Mr. McGuirk muttered something under his breath, and the men chuckled.

"It seems," Tom said, interpreting, "that he doesn't like us much. He doesn't like the food, and he doesn't like the beds. He says just when he got a good place fixed up in the coal cellar, Flannigan found it, and is asleep there now, this minute."

Aunt Selina rose suddenly and cleared her throat.

"Am I to understand," she asked severely, "that from now on we will have to add two newspaper reporters, three policemen and a burglar to the occupants of this quarantined house? Because, if that is the case, I absolutely refuse to feed them."

But one of the reporters stepped forward and bowed ceremoniously.

"Madam," he said, "I thank you for your kind invitation, but — it will be impossible for us to accept. I had intended to break the good news earlier, but this little game of burglar-in-a-corner prevented me. The fact is, your Jap has been discovered to have nothing more serious than chicken-pox, and — if you will forgive a poultry yard joke, there is no longer any necessity for your being cooped up."

Then he retired, quite pleased with himself.

One would have thought we had exhausted our capacity for emotion, but Jim said a joyful emotion was so new that we hardly knew how to receive it. Everyone shook hands with everyone else, and even the nurse shared in the excitement and gave Jim the medicine she had prepared for Tom.

Then we all sat down and had some champagne, and while

they were waiting for the police wagon, they gave some to poor McGuirk. He was still quite shaken from his experience when the dumb-waiter stuck. The wine cheered him a little, and he told his story, in a voice that was creaky from disuse, while Tom held my hand under the table.

He had had a dreadful week, he said; he spent his days in a closet in one of the maids' rooms — the one where we had put Jim. It was Jim waking out of a nap and declaring that the closet door had moved by itself and that something had crawled under his bed and out of the door, that had roused the suspicions of the men in the house — and he slept at night on the coal in the cellar. He was actually tearful when he rubbed his hand over his scrubby chin, and said he hadn't had a shave for a week. He took somebody's razor, he said, but he couldn't get hold of a portable mirror, and every time he lathered up and stood in front of the glass in the dining room sideboard, some one came and he had had to run and hide. He told, too, of his attempts to escape, of the board on the roof, of the home-made rope, and the hole in the cellar, and he spoke feelingly of the pearl collar and the struggle he had made to hide it. He said that for three days it was concealed in the pocket of Jim's old smoking coat in the studio.

We were all rather sorry for him, but if we had made him uncomfortable, think of what he had done to us. And for him to tell, as he did later in court, that if that was high society he would rather be a burglar, and that we starved him, and that the women had to dress each other because they had no lady's maids, and that the whole lot of us were in love with one man, it was downright malicious.

The wagon came for him just as he finished his story, and we all went to the door. In the vestibule Aunt Selina suddenly remembered something, and she stepped forward and caught the poor fellow by the arm.

"Young man," she said grimly. "I'll thank you to return what you took from *me* last Tuesday night."

McGuirk stared, then shuddered and turned suddenly pale.

"Good Lord!" he ejaculated. "On the stairs to the roof! *You?*"

They led him away then, quite broken, with Aunt Selina

staring after him. She never did understand. I could have explained, but it was too awful.

On the steps McGuirk turned and took a farewell glance at us. Then he waved his hand to the policemen and reporters who had gathered around.

"Good-bye, fellows," he called feebly. "I ain't sorry, I ain't. Jail'll be a paradise after this."

And then we went to pack our trunks.

NOTE FROM MAX WHICH CAME
THE NEXT DAY WITH ITS ENCLOSURE.

My Dear Kit —

The enclosed trunk tag was used on my trunk, evidently by mistake. Higgins discovered it when he was unpacking and returned it to me under the misapprehension that I had written it. I wish I had. I suppose there must be something attractive about a fellow who has the courage to write a love letter on the back of a trunk tag, and who doesn't give a tinker's damn who finds it. But for my peace of mind, ask him not to leave another one around where I will come across it. Max.

WRITTEN ON THE BACK OF THE TRUNK TAG.

Don't you know that I won't see you until tomorrow? For Heaven's sake, get away from this crowd and come into the den. If you don't I will kiss you before everybody. Are you coming? T.

WRITTEN BELOW.

No indeed.

K.

THIS WAS SCRATCHED OUT AND BENEATH.

Coming.

Printed in the United States
23914LVS00005B/298